THE NEW LEAF

THE NEW LEAF

Hugh Canham

Book Guild Publishing
Sussex, England

First published in Great Britain in 2013 by
The Book Guild Ltd
The Werks
45 Church Road
Hove, BN3 2BE

Typesetting in Baskerville by
Ellipsis Digital Ltd, Glasgow

Printed and bound in Great Britain by
CPI Group (UK) Ltd, Croydon, CR0 4YY

A catalogue record for this book is available from
The British Library.

ISBN 978 1 84624 968 6

1

I have been going over in my mind the strange things that have happened to me during the past year. In twelve months my life has changed beyond all recognition.

First, I see myself with Zoë in New York last Christmas walking hand-in-hand in the freezing cold down Fifth Avenue and buying hot chestnuts. She was wearing a fake black fur coat and earmuffs to match; her cheeks were pink with the cold.

And then, by contrast in Los Angeles at the New Year, swimming with her in the hotel pool under the palm trees and lying side-by-side and holding hands on the pool loungers as we dried off in the sun. She had on a minute bikini. And the next day in our room, when she announced that she wasn't coming back with me to England.

I was in bed hoping she would soon join me, but she just sat at the dressing table brushing her long, blonde hair.

'But sweetheart,' I said, 'I've got to go back tomorrow. I've got to get this deal finalised, I need the money. Can't you come back with me for a few days – a week at most – and then if you like, we'll fly back here?'

'No, Greg. I'm staying right here. I see a lot of opportunities!'

I got out of bed. I was naked, and went over to the dressing table and stood behind her. I gently put my hands over her breasts and then kissed the side of her neck. Normally this had the desired effect; but this time she shrugged me away and said, 'You're not going to get round me. I've made up my mind.'

I looked at all 6 foot 2 inches of myself towering over her in the mirror. My James Bond image, carefully cultivated for the last twenty-five years, hadn't faded too much. My hair wasn't going grey, either on my head or chest or elsewhere. My facial expression was suitably ruthless and my body looked reasonably fit, although I was perhaps putting on a bit of weight. What was happening? Why didn't she want me anymore?

'Okay. If that's the way you feel,' I said crossly and went into the bathroom, slamming the door behind me. I had a cold shower. I needed it.

When I came back into the bedroom, Zoë was sprawled in the middle of the bed, fast asleep in the black silk nightdress I had bought her in New York.

I didn't feel like moving her to get into bed. I went to my suitcase and took out the half bottle of Famous Grouse whisky I always carry with me when I'm travelling – I'm a bit mean about paying hotel prices for drinks – and poured myself a stiff one. I drew back the blinds a little and sat by the window, looking out over LA at night. The restaurant that had been on the corner of the road when I last stayed at the hotel had been demolished and some new erection was already shooting up in its place. Such is the way in Los Angeles.

Zoë was only nineteen and a model, so I could see her point of view. But I knew I was effectively being 'dumped' for the first time in my life.

Just after my forty-fifth birthday too. And at a time when I was getting distinctly nervous about my finances. I had been spending recklessly and I was going to have to borrow most of the money to do the next deal. I also suspected that my tax affairs were in a mess – my accountants would never give me a straight answer when I asked about them.

I didn't feel very well on the flight back to London. I think I had drunk too much. I was very upset about Zoë. She was lovely. Heathrow Airport looked like hell, shrouded in a thick fog with melting slush everywhere. God knows how the plane managed to land.

Early the next day, still a bit jet-lagged, I had this meeting with my old friend/foe, Jasper Cohen, at his sumptuous office just off Regent Street.

'Aha, had a good festive season Greg, by the looks of it! The States, wasn't it?'

For the third time, I was buying one of the companies which it seemed was surplus to his empire. My head throbbed during the negotiations, even after two large cups of black coffee. I looked at myself in the mirror in Jasper's opulent marble-lined loo as I went to have a pee. God, I did look pretty awful! Bags under my eyes and a yellowish complexion. I put my tongue out and then quickly put it in again – I suspected this was more than a hangover and jetlag.

I gritted my teeth and got on with the deal. Jasper could be so infuriating. He sat there grinning and massaging his great fat gut which was nearly bursting the bottom button of his shirt. Because of my throbbing head I think I let him get away with a few things I shouldn't have. I didn't feel in a fighting mood.

The company I was buying had three freehold shops, all well situated and with living accommodation over, a large warehouse and a so-so leasehold Head Office near Baker Street. I'd inspected them all before making Jasper an offer and more or less sold on two of the shops to a property dealer I knew, which should make me a £200,000 profit straight away. I had no intention of running the company. I was buying it to sell off its assets. Unfortunately, it had fifteen employees and its Managing Director was sitting beside Jasper, looking pretty sour about the whole thing. No doubt the poor sod was wondering where he would end up! Why he was working in Jasper's rombustious organisation, God only knew. Dressed in a black three-piece suit, he was about 7 feet tall, thin as a rake and very serious. Probably an accountant. He was going to be a problem and I'd have to discuss him with Jasper afterwards. He would undoubtedly cost a lot to get rid of; the other fourteen were just an annoying detail.

Why didn't Jasper sell off the company assets himself? Something to do with his tax position, apparently.

'Another striptease act?' he asked as he was showing me out.

'Could be,' I replied, smiling through a slight wave of nausea. 'We must have a word later on the phone about the MD.'

But first I called my lawyers so that I could go and see them and instruct them on the deal. I always liked to get things done quickly, once terms have been agreed. Then I called my secretary, Gloria. Through the ringing tone I imagined her sitting at her desk in my office's reception area tossing her hennaed locks, filing her nails and wreathed with fumes from her Rive Gauche perfume.

'Darling, it's me. What's the name of that doctor in Harley Street that everyone goes to these days?'

'Greg, are you ill!?'

'I don't know. I just want a check-up.'

'Dr Smith. Unusual, isn't it? I'll give you his number. He's apparently particularly good on urogenital diseases.'

'It's not that,' I snapped.

Gloria could be very cheeky.

As I punched in Dr Smith's number walking up Regent Street, I realised I was frightened.

4

My solicitors' offices are on the twenty-third floor of one of those City tower blocks. When it was built, the fashion was to have double glazed windows from ceiling to floor. I dislike the place. You can see vague reflections of yourself in the glass.

I had difficulty concentrating on giving instructions to George, the fat but amiable partner I deal with. His private office is very small and of course he had to have his assistant and a trainee present. I was seated right next to one of the windows and kept having an irresistible desire to look down at the road below. Each time I did it my stomach turned over – it was completely different from looking out of an aeroplane window. I suppose the fear of falling from a great height comes to everyone from time to time and that afternoon I was having it badly!

I kept having visions of Zoë's naked body while George talked about technical legal details. When I wasn't thinking I was falling into space or visualising the naked Zoë, I was worrying about going to see the doctor.

'I hope you don't mind me saying, you don't look that well today, Greg,' George said as we parted.

'No, I'm going for a check-up this afternoon.'

'Good. I hope everything's all right!'

By late afternoon, I was sitting in Dr Smith's waiting room; he had 'fitted me in'. I've always been afraid of doctors and this one appeared very formidable, sitting behind an exceptionally large desk in a grand consulting room as I was shown into his presence by an elegant, uniformed nurse.

'Tell me why you've come to see me.' He was rather brusque and smelled strongly of aftershave; probably about fifty-five, short hair, horn-rimmed spectacles and a very expensive-looking grey suit.

I told him. He went through the rigmarole of examining me and asking me a lot of questions. He looked into my ears, down my throat, into my eyes and tapped my knees with one of those long-handled hammers. He slapped his hand on my stomach. 'Bit flabby, aren't you?' he said smugly. I didn't take to him.

I was then handed over to another nurse – small and dumpy – who led me into a little room where she took my blood pressure and then wired me up to an ECG machine. Finally, she took blood samples. I'm terrified of needles, they always hurt, and I looked away when I saw my dark red blood oozing into the tube. I was asked to give a specimen of urine. It did look a bad colour – sort of darkish browny-yellow.

Then Dr Smith saw me again. This, I soon realised, was 'crunch time'.

'Tell me, how much do you drink?'

'Well... er...'

'Please be frank and specific otherwise I cannot make a proper diagnosis. What have you had to drink during the last few days?'

'I'm feeling a bit jet-lagged,' I said, 'but I'll do my best.' I could hardly remember, but I admitted to roughly half of what I'd had in LA and on the plane and since I'd been back.

He made a note.

'Smoke?'

'No cigarettes. Just cigars.'

'How many a day?'

'Two, maybe three.'

'Size?'

'Oh, you know, those Romeo and Juliet things.'

'No, I don't! Show me how long.'

'Um... about four to five inches.'

He made another note.

'Exercise?'

'Well, I'm a businessman. I don't have much spare time.'

'I see. Well, I should have the results of the blood tests by tomorrow afternoon. Make an appointment with my reception please to come and see me then after two-thirty, and we'll have a further talk.'

He looked at me stonily through those horn-rimmed spectacles. Obviously he didn't approve of my lifestyle.

'Oh God,' I thought, 'I'd better stay in for once this evening,' as I took a taxi back to Brook Street, thinking on the way that I should have walked to get a bit of exercise. But I was feeling awfully tired.

'Just cancel the dinner at the Casino,' I told Gloria, who was indeed haloed in Rive Gauche, but actually doing something on her computer. 'Say I'm not feeling well.'

'Aren't you really?'

'No, don't I look it?'

'Um... Well, few of us look our best after the festive season.'

I ignored this remark and didn't even bother to stop and ask about my messages. I went straight up in the lift to my flat. It was nearly six and I would have normally had a glass of champagne and then a bath, but instead I made myself a cup of black coffee and sat on the sofa looking out of the window at the bare plane trees outside, lit up by the street lamps against the night sky. I switched on the television and watched the news. Somebody had been murdered; the rest was not very interesting. Over the newsreader's voice, I could hear my ghastly old nanny telling me off, 'You're a naughty boy, Gregory, and one of these days it will catch up with you!'

Leaving Dr Smith's surgery the following afternoon, I headed north across the Marylebone Road into Regents Park. I had my thick overcoat on. I don't think it was particularly cold, but I felt as though I was walking somewhere near the Arctic. I sat down on a park bench and kept going over in my mind what the doctor had said: 'Of course, it's up to you, but in my opinion if you don't change your lifestyle you're going to be seriously ill in the near future! The tests show that you are drinking too much alcohol. Your blood pressure is very high, so is your cholesterol and there are irregularities in your ECG.'

A vision of that bloody nanny came into my mind again, wagging her finger at me, and coming out with another of her favourite phrases: 'Gregory, you've got to turn over a *new leaf!*'

So I replied to the doctor, 'You mean I've got to turn over a new leaf!?'

He seemed to thaw a little at this.

'Well, that sort of thing,' he said, smiling. 'It would be a good idea if you could give up alcohol completely for the time being, but if you can't do that, you should try to limit yourself to twenty-one units per week. I'll give you a sheet of paper which sets out exactly what that means. If you must smoke, only have one cigar a day and for goodness sake take some exercise. Walk, go swimming, join a gym.'

It was going to be very difficult to start a new regime immediately. My lawyers were meeting with Jasper's lawyers tomorrow at my office and I hoped to sign the share sale agreement. Then, in the evening, I was looking forward to a little dinner I'd set up with a few business acquaintances. The day after that was Saturday and one of my horses was running at Sandown – he stood a good chance of being placed, so I'd have to be there… The new-leaf turning would have to wait until Sunday. But as a token of my resolve, I walked all the way from Regents Park back to Brook Street and felt much warmer when I got there.

'How did it go?' asked Gloria.

'Oh, not too bad.'

'Stay off the booze, I suppose?'

'Yes, that sort of thing.'

Gloria really was very decorative and I loved seeing her sitting in my reception area, but she could be very irritating!

I went straight into my office and tried to concentrate on some computer printouts of the stock of the company I was buying from Jasper.

Why do lawyers always look so bloody miserable and carry such large bags? George came with not one but two assistants; both with enormous bags. I was very glad I'd agreed an overall fee in advance. George had wanted to charge me by the hour and no doubt those two assistants would be costing me £250 per hour each! Jasper's lot looked as though they'd come straight out of a synagogue, although I know Jasper himself is not religious. He told me. I think his exact words were: 'Load of bloody bullshit!' However, I supposed it was tribal loyalty. One of his blokes had one of those skullcaps held in place with a hairclip and he did actually smile a bit. The other three (two of them must have been accountants to safeguard Jasper's tax position, no doubt) were as glum as my 'team', as they will call themselves.

I had, of course, been through all the draft documents with George the previous day and made a list of the points to watch. The two things that worried me most were: (a) the fate of the Managing Director, and (b) the amount of stock the company was carrying in its warehouse and shops. I had agreed with Jasper that I would take the stock at cost, which was the normal sort of thing, but when I'd first studied the computer printouts which he'd sent me I was very worried. The stock was worth nearly a million – roughly twice what I thought it would be, and unbelievably there were 10,000 teddy bears! Yes, it was a company that imported and sold toys called 'Toy Boy Limited'. One of Jasper's little jokes, no doubt. He was very fond of jokes!

'Jasper,' I said on the phone (I was not feeling at my best, part of my brain mulling on turning over the new leaf), 'the stock figure is about twice what I'd expected!'

'Yes, we're well stocked, aren't we!' he replied, chuckling.

'But for God's sake, ten thousand teddies. Is this for *next* Christmas?'

'Er, no... '

'How the hell did you get so many teddy bears?'

'Well, there was a mistake!'

'Yes… '

'Yes.'

'By your highly-paid MD, no doubt?'

'Something like that.'

'So you want me to buy your expensive MD and his bloody mistake?'

'The company comes as it is.'

'Or not!'

'Come on, Greg, we've agreed terms. Stock at cost!'

'Why didn't you sack him?'

'He's got six kids.'

Jasper's a mean sod, but he has a bit of a soft centre.

'I see. So I've got to take on ten thousand teddy bears, a fool of an MD and his six kids!'

'Greg, be reasonable!'

This went on for some time.

At last, Jasper said, 'If you take the stock including the teddies, I'll keep the MD. I'll put him in charge of the share sale agreement and tell him if he does well I'll transfer him to another of my companies. I happen to have a vacancy anyhow!'

'Okay,' I said, reluctantly.

I had, of course, to ask the bank to increase its loan facilities by £500,000. They didn't seem too keen.

'Look,' I said to the manager, an old friend, 'I promise I'll sell the stock ASAP; moreover, I've got a buyer lined up for two of the freehold shops which will show a profit of two hundred thousand over their book value!'

Eventually, the bank very reluctantly agreed.

So in addition to Jasper's lawyers and accountants, the

said MD, apparently called Horace, presented himself in my
board room at 10 o'clock on Friday morning to supervise
the share sale agreement on Jasper's behalf. He looked
positively bursting with self-importance and pleasure. He
had on what was obviously a brand new three-piece suit –
dark blue this time. But he looked very sour again when I,
as is my invariable practice, retired from the meeting after
about five minutes, having explained that if they wanted me
for anything they should just ask Gloria, who would contact
me. This was why I liked to hold these meetings in my own
office. Gloria would be dealing with any amendments to the
agreement anyhow – I hate listening to lawyers arguing over
obscure and footling points. I wanted to get on and try to
unload some of the stock, particularly the teddy bears.

The worst feature of asset stripping is that you're always
lumbered with things you know nothing about – like toys.
It wasn't long, however, after I'd settled down in my office
that I had a message from George calling me into the board
room to discuss some trivial point. After I'd dealt with that,
I took him out into the hallway and in no uncertain terms
told him not to trouble me with anything unless it was world-
shattering.

'I pay you to protect me, so please get on with it. I'm very
busy.'

There were no further interruptions as I continued to
phone various toy wholesalers. By about twelve o'clock I'd
made absolutely nil progress, I was getting angry and needed
a drink, all the more so because I knew I shouldn't have one.
I called Gloria into my office.

'Look, darling, you're going to have to help me with this
sale of the stock. You've got nieces and nephews I know, so
you must know something about toy shops. Ring round a few
and see if any of them are interested in buying teddy bears.

'Right,' said Gloria, 'how big are they and how many?'

'Well, all the print-out says is 10,000 – various sizes.'

'Quite a few for one shop to buy!'

'Yes, of course!' (Oh God! It sounded as though Gloria was going into one of her sulks.) 'Just ask if they'd be interested in some, and you'd better order me a sandwich as I seem to be stuck here. And you'd better see if those guys in the board room want some, but lay off the prawns, ham and pork.'

'I'd have never thought of that!!' said Gloria, eyeing me frigidly. (Yes, definitely, she was going into a sulk.)

By five o'clock I'd only been summoned once more by George and I'd found two wholesalers who might be interested in about a hundred teddies each. Gloria said she hadn't had any time to ring anyone. She'd been too busy processing the amendments to the share sale agreement and getting sandwiches and cups of tea and coffee. I don't believe she'd tried very hard!

At seven o'clock Gloria informed me that 'They were ready for me,' and I followed my usual routine. Armed with a copy of the *Evening Standard* which I was scanning intently, I entered the board room and sat down.

'Now, is everything agreed?' I asked.

'Yes,' said George.

I looked round the meeting and said very forcefully, 'Has anyone got any points to raise before I sign? Anything at all?'

'There is one thing, sir,' said the Managing Director.

'Ah... and what is that?'

'Mr Cohen has just offered me another job within his organisation and if it's all right with you, sir, I should like my name deleted from the list of employees you are taking over with the company.'

I restrained myself from smiling.

'If that's what you'd prefer,' I said, somewhat coldly, 'it's fine by me.'

So we deleted his name and both signed the document and initialled the deletion. As was my custom, I briefly nodded to everyone and left.

'Never thank any of them,' my father used to say, 'they'll only try and charge you extra!'

I'd taken a shower during the afternoon and my friend Tina was, as arranged, in the reception waiting to be taken out to the dinner. Gloria was chatting to her rather icily. Tina looked magnificent. She had on red shoes with heels about 5 inches high, skin-tight black trousers and a very low-cut white top out of which her huge bosom looked in imminent danger of escape. Her long, blonde hair lay on her shoulders.

'Sorry if I've kept you waiting, sweetheart,' I said as I sat down very close to her on one of the big white sofas in the reception. 'I've just been finalising a deal.'

The weary-looking lawyers and accountants straggled out of the board room clutching their heavy briefcases, through the reception and out of the front door casting, I thought, longing eyes both on Tina and Gloria and no doubt going home to their boring wives and children.

2

I'd taken Tina out a couple of times previously and I was hoping she would provide a good substitute for Zoë. She was sexy and funny – particularly when she'd had a few drinks. But was she temperamental, and this evening particularly so! The dinner party with a few business acquaintances was in a private room in a restaurant in Jermyn Street. You always hope something may come from these dos. Five of us chip in a bit each and ask some friends. I was feeling very happy, having bought Toy Boy Limited and unburdened myself of the morose Managing Director, but Tina was distinctly 'off'. While we were all having a glass or two of champagne before sitting down, I put my arm around her hips and gently stroked her bum. She had seemed to quite like that sort of thing, even in public places, but tonight she flounced away immediately and stood three paces away glaring at me.

'Do you know your breath smells?' she hissed.

How do you reply to that? Tina moved away and when we all sat down (it was very informal), she plonked herself down between a wheeler-dealer called Roger and a lecherous old bugger unbelievably called Jesu, who both seemed very pleased with the arrangement. When I had recovered from this slight, I found myself having to fill the only vacant chair between Belinda and a rather plain girl I'd never seen before.

Having had nothing to drink for two days, the three

glasses of champagne I'd slurped down before dinner had rather gone to my head. Also, I was very hungry after the frustrations of trying to sell teddy bears.

'You don't know anyone who wants to buy an awful lot of teddy bears, do you?' I asked the rather plain girl.

'Er… no,' she said pursing her lips. 'What an odd thing to ask. Do you sell toys?'

'Not usually,' I said, 'but I am at the moment.'

Scanning the table, I still couldn't make out which of my acquaintances the girl had come with. I didn't like to ask her as I felt I'd made one false start already and she was obviously rather prim! Not for her the plunging cleavage. She had on a plain black skirt and a white blouse which was fastened closely at the neck with a small brooch. As the blouse was a sort of loose-fitting, billowing affair, it was impossible for me to see what her bust was like, or indeed if she even had one. There were about twenty of us altogether. Belinda, on my left, I knew quite well. She was the long-standing mistress of a property developer, who sat winking at me (or was it at her?) from the other side of the table. His wife was also there. How do people get away with these things?

'Do you know this girl on my right?' I whispered to Belinda, trying to direct my supposedly bad breath away from her nostrils.

Belinda, who had her reading glasses on at the time and was suspiciously surveying what the waiter had brought her, peered past me over her glasses, glared at the young lady and said in a loud voice, 'No, Greg, never set eyes on her before!'

I can't remember much about the rest of the evening. Belinda, I think, got up and left early. I remember having a large Armagnac and then the rest is a blank.

I surfaced in a strange bed in a strange bedroom. It was dark. I felt around my body. I had my underwear on. I badly needed a pee. Somebody must have helped me to bed. This was terrible! In a lifetime of late parties I'd never not made it home before. I sat up slowly and tried to get up. Then I lay down again – very quickly. The bedroom was rotating, then a door opened and a female form dressed in white entered and turned on the light. 'Oh God, it's a nurse,' I thought, 'I've been taken to hospital.' I tried to focus on the female form. It slowly resolved itself to someone who looked rather like the girl on my right-hand side the night before. She wasn't wearing a nurse's uniform. She was in a white dressing gown.

'How are you feeling?' she said. Yes, it was definitely her.

'I think I may come round in a minute or two.'

'Would a cup of black coffee help?'

'Yes, please.'

'Sugar?'

'No thanks. Here, wait a minute. How did I get here?'

'You don't remember?'

'Obviously not.'

'I'll tell you when I come back with the coffee.'

While she was gone I tried to look at my watch, which was still on my wrist. It seemed to be ten o'clock. Then I remembered 'Sir Will' was running at Sandown. I *had* to be there. Racing started at twelve forty-five. He was in the two-thirty, so I must get home and change as quickly as possible!

'Now you'll feel much better when you've drunk this. Just let me prop you up a bit with this extra pillow.'

After half a cup of her coffee, I felt much better. It was very strong and black.

'Look, I must get up. I need to go to the loo, and I've got to get to Sandown races. I've a horse running.'

'That's good. But don't you want to know how you got here?'

'Of course, later. But I must get home and change and get to Sandown by one-thirty at the latest. His race is at two-thirty. Where are we now, by the way?'

'Quite near last night's restaurant.'

'But how near?'

'Knightsbridge.'

'Oh good.'

'So you're close to your home?'

'Yes, I live in Brook Street. But why am I here?'

'You seemed – well, a little disorientated shall we say, and nobody left at the dinner knew exactly where you lived. So I said I'd bring you here. It's not far.'

'How did we get here?'

'I couldn't get a taxi so we walked. But you did stagger quite a bit, particularly round Hyde Park Corner!'

'You're very kind!' I hoped silently that I'd behaved myself. I know I'm given to bottom-pinching and other antisocial behaviour when drunk.

'I couldn't leave you all alone in the restaurant at nearly midnight, now could I? Not after you'd been so nice to me all evening.'

'Was I?'

'Very.'

'Ah… good!'

'And you kept kissing me!'

I didn't ask for any further details, but obviously my breath wasn't all that repulsive! Then I had a thought…

'How would you like to come to the races with me,' I said, 'as a reward for looking after me?'

I was sure she was going to look prim and turn me down but to my surprise she said she'd love to.

We arrived at Sandown just as the second race was starting. Jane, for that was her name, didn't seem at all impressed with my Aston Martin. She made rather a fuss about lowering herself into it and took off a rather silly knitted woollen hat she was wearing once she was inside. But she did appear to know about horses and patted Sir Will in his box while he was being saddled. Normally he doesn't like strangers but he didn't seem to mind Jane. My totally neurotic trainer, Jim, muttered out of the corner of his mouth, 'Strewth, where'd you get 'er from... not yer usual!!'

I just smiled and shrugged and asked, 'What price are we?'

'Six to one; seven to one some places. We stand a good chance, at least of a place.'

From Jim, that was optimism.

It was bitterly cold and I felt like a very large whisky and something to eat. But there wasn't time.

'I shall put something on Sir Will – yes I will,' said Jane as we stood in the parade ring. Sir Will did indeed look in good condition as he walked round. I couldn't really figure out Jane. During our car ride she told me she'd lived in her flat off Knightsbridge for a year, which I thought very wealthy for such a young girl. She must only be about twenty-three or twenty-four. Her father lived in the country. Mummy was dead and she didn't have any brothers or sisters. She didn't know exactly what she wanted to do yet; she'd only just finished at university.

As I walked up the steps to the area reserved for owners and trainers and watched the twelve runners go down to the post, I noticed Jane standing about 20 yards away. She'd left us to go and put a bet on and she obviously didn't like to come into the owners' and trainers' section without being invited. She looked a strange little figure, I thought, with her tweed overcoat, woolly hat, and some rimless spectacles which she'd just put on. I thought it best to leave her where she was as I wanted to concentrate on watching the race through my binoculars. Jim made awful grunting and gurgling noises beside me. He always did this during a race when one of his horses was running.

It was a 2-mile chase so they set off at a cracking pace up the hill. Sir Will was in the lead at the first ditch.

'Silly bugger,' muttered Jim – this was aimed at the jockey – 'I told him to keep off the pace!'

Then some moments later at the water jump where Sir Will was still in front, 'Stupid fool! He's sure to make a muck of the Railway fences with nobody in front of him!'

Sure enough, Sir Will duly hit the top of the first Railway fence pretty hard and was headed for the first time. He also made a mess of the second Railway fence and that put him back in fourth place.

'Oh Christ, he's finished now!' moaned Jim beside me. 'The stupid cunt, I'll never let him ride for me again!'

It certainly looked to me as if Sir Will would finish out of the first three. But rounding the final bend and coming to the Pond fence, Sir Will got a second wind. He jumped the Pond fence into third place and drew up alongside the two leaders at they toiled up the Sandown Hill.

Jim had fallen silent. Then as the three horses approached the final fence and jumped it in a line, he bellowed beside my left ear, nearly causing permanent injury,

'Come on my son!!'

As usual, I uttered a prayer to Allah (I've often found they work) and Sir Will duly came first by half a length.

'Thank Christ for that!' uttered Jim, scampering down the steps. 'Come on, Greg!'

But something was gripping my arm. It was Jane's hand.

'Wonderful!' she said. 'What a wonderful race, wasn't it? Congratulations!'

Jim didn't seem to think the jockey was such a cunt any longer as he dismounted in the winners' enclosure. He threw his arms around him.

I collected a rather nice silver cup which I gave to Jim for safekeeping and then looked round for Jane. Eventually I found her sitting on the bench beneath a tree, by the paddock. This seemed a very odd place to be as there was a freezing cold wind and it had just started to snow. Almost everyone else had disappeared inside.

'Come on,' I said, patting her shoulder jovially, 'let's spend some of my winnings on some champagne and maybe something to eat. I hope you put a lot on him, I certainly did.'

But she didn't seem at all keen. 'I don't usually drink during the day,' she said.

'Oh come on, it's nearly dark already,' I said. 'There are only two more races and at this rate they'll need floodlighting for the last one. Just something to eat then?'

'Okay, if you like.'

We found a table in the ground floor restaurant and I could hardly wait for the champagne to arrive. I did eventually persuade Jane to have one glass with her fish while we watched the next race on one of the monitors in the restaurant. Jane was silent throughout. We could hardly see the race – it started to snow very hard just after the off.

'Bet the last will be cancelled!' I said.

And then I caught sight of two very lovely young ladies coming into the restaurant. One was dark and the other blonde, undoubtedly both enhanced by their respective hairdressers, and I was very pleased when I realised that I was vaguely aquainted with the dark girl. She was the daughter of another trainer I had a couple of horses with. They removed scarves, coats and hats and sat down at a table almost next to us. I waved.

'Well, hello there, Greg,' she called out. 'Congratulations! Are you treating us to champagne after your win?'

'Yes, yes, of course,' I said, 'come and join us. There are two more places here. Er... it's Lucy, isn't it?'

'That's right! And this is Katherine.'

'This is Jane.'

'Howdy!' said Katherine.

I poured them out some champagne and ordered another bottle.

'Wonderful race, Greg,' said Lucy grasping and squeezing one of my hands.

'Yes, wasn't it!'

'The final race on the card has been abandoned owing to the deteriorating weather conditions,' the loudspeaker announced.

'Oh God,' said Lucy, 'and I was hoping to have put a big bet on that!'

'Yip, we were, weren't we Lucy?'

'I think I'll be going,' Jane said.

'Oh, but the fun is only just starting!' I said.

'Yes... well!'

'Oh, Jane, there's a party tonight. Why don't you and Greg join us? It's at my sister's place in Fulham.'

'No, thank you for asking but I must go,' said Jane.

'Well, I'm sorry,' I said gallantly to Lucy and her friend, 'I'll have to take Jane home.'

'No, there's absolutely no need for that. I'll get the train. I insist. The walk to the station will do me good.'

'But, please... ' I said, standing up.

She gently pushed me down again.

'No, I must go home,' she said.

I was feeling very comfortable and didn't want to argue.

'Well, if you insist.'

'Thank you for asking me to come with you,' she said and purposefully strode out of the restaurant into the snow, donning her woolly hat. From the direction she took it seemed as if she was intent on walking across the racecourse to the station. Oh well! I shrugged my shoulders and smiled reassuringly at Lucy and her friend and poured us all another glass of champagne. Lucy raised an eyebrow.

'Strange girl, Greg. Known her long?'

'Er... yes, maybe, and no, to the two parts of your question.'

'Vaguely familiar. What's her surname?'

'Do you know, she never told me. I only met her yesterday evening.'

'I see,' said Lucy and giggled.

We sat awhile drinking and then it started to snow even harder so we decided to leave our cars in the car park and go back to London by train. I have to admit it was not entirely due to the snow, as we were all rather inebriated. I have always loved a fall of snow; this one was particularly beautiful because as the snow stopped, the clouds cleared and a full moon appeared low in the sky. It was so bright, it lit up our path across the racecourse to the station.

As we started walking, Katherine kept waving her arms in the air and shouting, 'Gee! This is just great.' Then she started throwing snowballs at me and Lucy joined in. No doubt because of the amount of champagne they'd drunk, their aim was very wide of the mark, thank goodness, and so eventually they gave up and came and walked either side of me with their arms linked through mine. As we got to the other side of the course, Lucy said she thought she'd try and jump one of the fences. I refused to let go of her arm and so we had a bit of a tussle, laughing and screaming, ending up in a small drift of snow at the edge of the course.

Opportunities for threesomes are rare and I remember I was beginning to feel hopeful as we got on the train together.

During the journey, Lucy lolled on one of my shoulders and Katherine on the other. Katherine had informed that she was 'into' horses as she came from Kentucky and insisted on singing snatches of some dreadful old song which started off, 'Down in old Kentucky where horseshoes are lucky.' She had a terrible voice! One line of the song which she kept repeating was, 'Bop down the Avenue.' When she came each time to the 'bop' she punched my arm or my chest very fiercely. Fortunately, the two other people in the compartment seemed to think it was funny!

We took a taxi from Waterloo to Lucy's flat in Fulham where she said we could have some 'tea' until the party started at eight-thirty. The tea consisted of a large slice of Christmas cake each and a bottle of red wine. Then Lucy suggested I might like to take a shower to freshen up before going to the party. This seemed like a good idea – and an even better one when Lucy and Katherine both joined me. I remember we soaped one another down and laughed a good deal. Then, when it was all about to get really interesting, Katherine slipped on a bar of soap and fell over and cut her face on the shower mechanism. I've never heard such foul language! Anyhow, that put an end to the shower and Lucy had to apply a plaster to Katherine's face, who swore even more when she realised it would spoil her 'chances' (as she put it) later in the evening.

The party was at Lucy's sister's flat nearby. My recollections are rather blurred. There were far too many people crammed into two small rooms. I remember having another glass or two of wine and a puff or two of a joint, then falling asleep on a sofa. It was very hot and noisy and I'd taken off my jacket and put it somewhere. I was woken up by noise from the next room – shouting, maybe fighting – followed by what sounded like a window being broken. There was a great deal of yelling and screaming, then police sirens outside. Somebody beside me said, 'Let's get out quick,' so I did – out of a back window and down the fire escape. From there I must have run down a series of alleys and out into the Fulham Road. The cold air sobered me up immediately, but I felt awfully sick and I think I vomited into the gutter. When I looked up, I could see the police car with its lights flashing outside the flat about 50 yards away, so I quickly set off in the opposite direction. Then it started to snow hard again and I only had on my trousers and shirt. I needed to get a taxi, but when I felt in my trouser pockets there was no money there at all. I'd have to ask the driver to wait when we got home and I'd get some money out of the safe. Oh bugger! Of course, the keys to my office and flat were in my jacket pocket and my mobile phone must have been in my overcoat, which I deposited somewhere at the beginning of the party. Oh shit, shit, shit.

Then an idea formed in my very fuddled brain. Of course, Cristabel! The exquisite Cristabel. Her studio must only be 200 yards away. I'd bought two of her very large and very expensive abstracts for my office. She'd been so grateful and said that she'd always be pleased to see me at her studio at any time.

But she didn't sound entirely pleased when she answered her entryphone. I think she must have been in bed.

'Who?' she asked, curtly.

'Gregory,' I said. 'You know! Gregory Bannister.'

'Oh yes! What do you want?'

I explained that I was standing outside in my shirt and trousers, had lost my keys and my money and my credit cards, was freezing cold and could I please come in. There was a pause.

'Okay, well then you'd better come up!' she said eventually.

The climb to her studio at the top of her eight-storey building was an effort, but when I saw her standing in the open doorway wearing a long white robe, it was all well worth it! It was like being greeted by a welcoming angel – except Cristabel had long, dark hair. And I think angels are supposed to be fair.

'Gregory, you look terrible,' she said. 'You'd better come in and lie down.'

Cristabel's only vice, as far as I knew, was smoking, otherwise she was totally calm, self-contained and apparently virtuous. She made me lie down on a settee in her studio, which doubled as a sitting room, covered me with a rug as I was shivering violently, sat down on a chair beside me and lit a cigarette.

'Tell me what's happened.'

I told her about my horse winning and gave her a somewhat expurgated account of the party.

'Quite a night!' she said. 'I can imagine what sort of party it was!'

'Oh, can you!?'

'Of course, I went to one or two of that sort when I was very young. Surely Gregory, if you don't mind my saying so, you should be getting past all that at your age.'

'Er... possibly.' I thought Cristabel looked very lovely albeit rather severe, but God, I wanted to go to sleep. My eyes must have closed and she noticed it.

'I suppose you'd better stay here for the night if you want, as you can't get into your flat. But hadn't you better do something about your credit cards?'

'Well I suppose in these days of chip and PIN it's unlikely anyone will use them. But I did write my PIN number in the front of my diary. Silly of me, wasn't it? They're all insured and I should inform the insurers – but of course I don't have their number. I expect my secretary will have it; I'll have to ring her first thing in the morning. And of course, she's got a set of keys to my office and flat.'

'Fine,' said Cristabel. 'Look Gregory, it's none of my business, but you don't look well. It doesn't look like just one bad party!'

'Well, yes. You're right. I've been to see the doctor and been advised to go a bit easier, but I was having a final fling. Tomorrow, I'm going to turn over a new leaf!'

'Good. Well, shall I make you a cup of tea? Coffee may keep you awake.'

'Yes, tea please,' I said. But I doubted if anything would keep me awake for long. The last thing I remember was admiring the way Cristabel walked away from me as she went to make the tea.

I awoke to bright sunshine streaming into the studio. For the second night running I looked around and wondered where I was. Then Cristabel appeared in her robe, just like Jane, carrying a cup of tea and saying I didn't drink the one she'd made last night, by the time she brought it to me I was fast asleep. So she'd just covered me up with two blankets and left me.

My mouth tasted awful and my head ached again, but I propped myself up, looked at Cristabel and thought she was the most beautiful thing I'd ever seen.

'You'd better drink this and then get on to your secretary. It's gone nine o'clock and she's probably awake. How do you feel?'

'Oh pretty good!' I said, although I didn't really – it was the day of the new leaf and I'd have to make an effort.

'Fine. Do you want to use my phone? I suppose you've lost your mobile as well as everything else?'

'Yes. But first I must use your bathroom.'

'Can't you go back to where the party was and try to retrieve all your stuff?'

'Well, the thing is, I'm not sure where it was exactly.'

'That *is* a difficulty,' said Cristabel – rather heavily, I thought.

I tried Gloria but all I got was her answering service. She'd probably gone away for the weekend. I'd have to try later but for now, I had to concentrate on the new leaf! I found Cristabel in her kitchen.

'I see,' she said when I told her that I couldn't get hold of Gloria. 'Would you like some more tea and some toast? I'm going to church in a few minutes and I'll leave you to have a bath or a shower. I'll be back in about an hour.'

Going to church!… Yes, Cristabel would. It went with the angelic look. I thought again of the new leaf, and anyhow I suppose I wanted to stay near her. And of course going to church on Sunday was a decent thing to do. My nanny had always insisted that we both went – every week.

'I'll come with you if you like!'

Cristabel's eyes opened wide. 'Really! Well you can't come like that. Your shirt and trousers look as if they've been slept in.'

'Ah yes! Well they have, haven't they?'

'But don't let it stop you. Go and have a quick wash. I haven't got a razor I'm afraid. But you can borrow one of my sloppy jumpers and an anorak.'

It turned out to be a Catholic church. I loathe Catholic churches. It never occurred to me that Cristabel was a Catholic. She surely wasn't Irish; she seemed rather upper-class English. And it was a dismal Catholic church too, with paint peeling from the walls and lots of yucky statues with candles burning in front of them. But to start off with there was some quite nice singing and a reading or two, and then the priest got up into the pulpit and started his sermon. He was an enthusiastic young bugger and he rattled on about Jesus's baptism and about sin and 'new starts' and that sort of thing. God, it sounded as if he knew this was the day I had to turn over a new leaf. But as he drivelled on, a gnawing sensation started in my guts and spread slowly up my chest. It seemed as though there was a balloon inside me trying to burst my ribcage. What on earth was happening to me? I breathed deeply and tried to control my body, but it was no use, I couldn't. I nudged Cristabel.

'I must go outside... need some fresh air... '

She nodded as though she understood and this was perfectly normal. But by the time I reached the back of the church I thought I was going to faint. Must get outside quickly... I tore down the long entrance porch and out into the sunlight. That was better! But the street was going up and down and I felt I was going to die. I sat down on the pavement and leant against the church wall...

3

I came round in a hospital. I was on a trolley and a nurse was beside me.

'You'll be okay,' she said, patting my arm reassuringly.

Then there was a blank; I was in a bed on a small ward and Cristabel was sitting on a chair beside the bed, looking at me. 'What happened?' I said.

'You passed out.'

'What's happening now, though?'

'They say they're assessing you.'

'I see. What day is it?'

'Sunday evening.'

'How long shall I be here for?'

'They won't say. But are you feeling a bit better now?'

'Yes, I suppose so.'

'Good. Well, I must go now.'

'Must you really? I've only just woken up!'

'I came here in the ambulance with you, I've been here ever since and I've got to go away first thing in the morning.'

'Where to?'

'Oh, just to see someone. That's all.'

'What about my keys and things?'

'I'm sorry, I haven't done anything about them. I didn't have your secretary's phone number.'

'I must phone her!'

'No, look – give me her number and if she doesn't answer, I'll leave her a message explaining what happened and telling her where you are.'

'Sodding hell!' I thought as I watched her walk away. At least I could still admire the way she moved. 'My last link with friends gone!' I didn't feel as bad as I had done in the church, but I certainly didn't feel very well.

A young Indian doctor came and spoke to me a bit later. He smiled a great deal, but I found his accent rather difficult to understand. Then three more doctors came to look at me. They drew the curtains round my bed and they took blood and urine samples and looked into my eyes, ears and mouth, etc. just like Dr Smith. Then they asked me interminable questions and made notes of my answers. How old was I? What sort of work did I do? Were my parents alive? As they weren't, what did they die of?... It was all very tiring. Then they got on to the drinking and smoking. I wasn't completely honest, I just said I smoked a couple of cigars a day and of course had quite a few drinks over Christmas and New Year. They nodded wisely. They asked had I any idea of what might have caused me to feel ill in the church and then to faint outside? Cristabel must have told somebody about all that when I was admitted. I said I had no idea. Once again they nodded wisely and left me with the third doctor. He was the youngest; he had a spotty face and seemed very nervous. He took my blood pressure and then sounded me all over with a stethoscope. I think he was probably only a student and they were letting him practise on me.

When they'd gone, a superior-looking nurse came and gave me an injection. I felt woozy and fell asleep. As I dropped off, I thought of Dr Smith's warning that I was heading for trouble. It seemed so unfair that it had happened just after I'd decided to turn over the new leaf.

The next morning they wheeled me down miles of

corridor and gave me an ECG, then wheeled me back into a new ward.

I hadn't been able to eat the breakfast and the lunch was decidedly unappetising. I was wondering what Gloria was doing about my cards and keys when a nurse wheeled a phone towards me on a trolley; Gloria was on the line.

'Got a message,' she said crisply, 'from a woman friend of yours that you were in hospital and you'd lost your keys, your credit cards, your mobile phone, all your money, and had passed out in the street.'

'Yes, that's right, darling,' I said, weakly. 'Are you coping with everything?'

'I'm doing my best. But how can you lose all those things at once?'

'I lost my jacket and overcoat.'

'Put them on a horse no doubt!'

'Look, Gloria, please be sympathetic. I'm in hospital.'

'I know; and it doesn't surprise me! Where did you lose your coat and jacket?'

'At a party. The police were called. Spot of bother. I bailed out quickly.'

'Hah… and straight into the arms of, what's she called?'

'Cristabel. She painted the pictures in reception.'

'Oh, those! Is she with you?'

'No, she had to go away. Will you come and see me please when you've sorted everything out? I'm rather lonely.'

'I may, when I have time. I'm still trying to sort out the mess. I wondered where you were when I came in this morning.'

'Thanks. But please come and see me!'

I put the phone back and pushed the trolley away from me. Obviously Gloria had moved from a sulk into a full-blown temper! It happened every six months or so. She said I was impossible, she was going to leave, etc. etc. etc. then after twenty-four hours she'd calm down. I dozed off again.

When I woke up a familiar face was peering anxiously at me. I blinked. It was plain Jane, minus her woolly hat and glasses.

'Jane, what the bloody hell are you doing here?'

'Gregory, that's not a very nice way to greet me when I've come to see to you!'

'How did you know I was here?'

'Well, this morning I made the bed you slept in and I found this.' She produced a small white envelope. 'I thought you might be very worried that you'd lost it, so, as I still didn't know where you live, I phoned your trainer and he gave me your office number, and your secretary – who seemed very cross, by the way – told me you'd collapsed and been taken to this hospital. So I thought I ought to come and see how you were and bring you the ring!'

'The ring?'

'Yes.'

She opened the envelope and took out a signet ring. Of course it was mine, but I hadn't missed it as I only wear it when I'm doing a deal. While negotiating it, I wear it on my ring finger, but once the deal's been done I move it onto my little finger as with the passing years it's become a little tight. It's a sort of lucky token. I'd obviously still had it on at the dinner.

'Thanks,' I said and looked at the engraving inside the ring.

'To G love from Mum.'

'Yes,' I said smiling wanly, 'it has some sentimental value but I don't always wear it, so I hadn't realised it was missing. But thank you so much – I should have been very sad if I'd lost it.'

'Is your mother still alive?'

'No. Both my parents are dead.'

'I see… Well, how do you feel?'

'Not too good, I'm afraid.'

'What happened exactly?'

'I don't really want to go into it. Apparently I passed out in the street having been to a church with a friend. I suppose it was somewhere near here.'

'Church?!'

'Yes. Don't sound so surprised. I don't go very often – in fact, hardly at all. But I've turned over a new leaf, you see.'

'Goodness! I hope that doesn't mean that you're going to be frightfully boring in the future!'

Somehow, Jane was a very reassuring presence to have at my bedside and I dozed off again. How long I'd been asleep I don't know, but Jane was still sitting beside me reading a book when I woke up.

'Is it still snowing?' I said.

'No. That was on Saturday. It was lovely on Sunday, today is Monday and it's quite nice, but still cold.

'What are you reading?'

'It's a Henry James novel, "The Spoils of Poynton".'

'I see!' It occurred to me that Jane was even stranger than I had at first thought.

'Do you like him?'

'Oh yes, very much indeed.'

Three of the other beds on the ward were empty; the men in the other two were asleep. As I dozed and Jane read, a mighty rushing wind disturbed the calm and Gloria stood at the end of my bed, glaring.

'Well, here I am,' she said. 'Goodness, you look awful!'

'Please don't shout, darling!' I glanced at Jane. She'd put down her book and looked faintly bewildered.

'This, Jane, is my secretary Gloria. Gloria, this is my friend Jane. I think you've spoken on the phone.'

'Yes, we have,' said Gloria, who as usual was looking glamorous, wearing a large fur coat and exuding clouds of her perfume.

'Darling, please speak more quietly or you'll wake the

other patients. Just pull up a chair and tell me what you've managed to do.'

Gloria reluctantly grabbed one of the plastic chairs scattered around the ward and placed it noisily on the opposite side of the bed from Jane. She removed her fur coat, threw it onto my bed, sat down and continued to glare at me.

'I've managed to put a stop on all your cards and ordered new ones. I've had the locks to the office changed by Banhams. Here are two new keys. And here are your spare car keys and a fifty pound note from the petty cash in case you need it. Nobody's broken into the office and flat, although I suppose your address must have been on the business cards in your pockets or in your diary. But the bad news is that the car seems to be missing from the underground car park. Yes, I checked.'

'Darling, you're the most efficient secretary anyone ever had. You've done wonderfully. Don't worry about the car; it's in the car park at Sandown racecourse. Look, you keep the car keys and perhaps you could pick it up tomorrow and drive it back to my parking for me. It's easy to get to Sandown by train from Waterloo.'

I thought she was going to go berserk.

'I'm not picking up your bloody car from Sandown,' she shouted. 'Wasting all that money on racehorses and betting!'

'But darling, Sir Will won. Forty thousand in prize money and I had a thousand pounds on him at seven to one. All tax free!'

I hadn't until that moment taken in the fact that this had considerably eased my immediate financial difficulties.

'That makes a change. It's a terrible waste of money, racing and betting, don't you think?' she said, addressing Jane for the first time, who she no doubt assumed was the last person likely to be interested in horse racing.

'Well, actually, no I don't,' said Jane. 'I was at the races on Saturday when Sir Will won and it was a most wonderful experience. It really was!'

'She was with you?' said Gloria, glaring at me.

'Yes… '

'In that case I suggest she picks up the car for you. If, of course, she can drive!'

'What a good idea!' said Jane, smiling. 'If you'd like to give me the keys, I'll do it first thing tomorrow. I remember the registration number; GRE22 isn't it? You'll tell me where you'd like me to park it?'

I wanted to laugh even though I felt so ill. Gloria was absolutely speechless at being outwitted. I'd never seen her nonplussed before. Well, Jane was full of surprises!

Gloria left shortly afterwards in a very black mood. I tried to get Jane to stay longer, but she said she had 'something to do'. Why is it that women are so bloody secretive? So I lay there feeling very sorry for myself.

By the next morning, the ward was full and another doctor came towards me, smiling.

'You may go now.'

'You mean, home, discharged?'

'That's right. Please get dressed.'

He started to draw the curtains around the bed.

'But what about the other tests?'

'No more tests at the moment.'

'But what about the results?'

'Don't worry, they'll be sent to your GP.'

I didn't know whether to be glad or sorry as I started slowly to put my crumpled clothes on. I found them stuffed in a locker beside my bed. I'd conditioned myself for staying in hospital for… well, I didn't really know, but certainly I hadn't thought I would be leaving so soon. I was glad to see that Cristabel's pullover and anorak were still with my other clothes.

'You all right?' A nurse peered in between my drawn curtains.

'I think so.' In fact I felt a bit light headed, but I wasn't going to let on. All I wanted to do now was to get out of the bloody place and into a taxi home. But as I walked slowly down the corridors of that vast hospital, it did occur to me that the reason I was being discharged was because they needed my bed for someone else. When they'd done my ECG I was sure they'd said they'd be doing a scan or something the next day...

There weren't any black cabs waiting outside, but as I wandered about wondering what to do a very dilapidated car drew up and a swarthy man with a large moustache stuck his head out of the window.

'Minicab, sir?'

Yes, that would do.

'Where to?'

I told him 'Brook Street, Mayfair', but he seemed to have no idea which way to go. He said he was Turkish – a student. He looked about fifty.

Eventually, with me giving him directions, we arrived at my office.

'How much?' I said.

'Thirty pounds, sir.'

It seemed an awful lot but I didn't want to argue. I offered the man the £50 note that Gloria had given me from the petty cash and said to take five for himself.

'No, sorry, don't take fifty pound notes, sir. Boss says may be forged!'

'Well, I'm afraid that's all I've got.'

'Got a credit card? We take Visa and Mastercard.'

'Ah, no... sorry!'

He peered round at me very suspiciously. No doubt I looked scruffy. I hadn't shaved since going into hospital.

'Maybe you go into that shop. Get some change?'

'No, no. You hold the fifty pounds and I'll go into my

office over there and get something smaller. I may be a few moments.'

I walked up to the rather splendid front door of my office, but it was shut! And there was no light on inside. Where the hell was Gloria! I fumbled in my trouser pockets for the keys.

'Burglar alarm! Burglar alarm!' sounded in my brain and I managed to punch in the number on the keypad as I entered. I made straight for Gloria's desk and opened the drawer where the petty cash box was. The box was there, but the key was not. Where did she keep the bloody thing? Never mind, I had several hundred pounds upstairs in the safe in my flat. But when I got to the safe (cunningly concealed in the back of my wardrobe), could I manage to work the combination? No. I tried five times then had to give up. Had Gloria changed it?

I went downstairs to explain things to the driver, but as I emerged from the front door I saw the dilapidated car driving away with my £50 note. Ah well, I'd only been overcharged by £15. In my present state of health I didn't really care. I shut and locked the office door from the inside and sat down wearily on one of my very nice leather sofas. I looked up at Cristabel's pictures and thought how beautiful she was. But what the hell had happened to Gloria? Perhaps she was ill. Then I saw an envelope propped up against her computer screen. I went over, grabbed it and tore it open;

'Dear Greg,

You won't be surprised; I've left. I'm sorry to do this while you're in hospital but you are really impossible to work with and I can't stand another day of it or else I shall go mad! There's a note on the computer explaining where everything is and what I have done and not done.

Gloria.'

'Oh triple shit,' I said, screwing the letter into a ball and throwing it into a corner. I went upstairs to my flat. All I felt like doing was lying on the bed. I was furious. Gloria must have known that as a matter of principle I couldn't and didn't ever use the computer; that's what a secretary's for! She'd put everything onto the computer and left it like that so I'd have to get help. Why hadn't she phoned me in the hospital to tell me she was leaving? It could have been days before I was discharged and the office meanwhile would have gone to rack and ruin! She'd probably left because of Jane and the car. It was all Jane's fault – had she brought the car back? And if so, where were the keys?

But after a time I decided that I couldn't just lie there feeling angry. I got up, tore off my awful crumpled clothes and staggered into the bathroom to look at myself in the mirror. What a mess! I virtually had a beard, in which I noticed were several grey hairs on either side of my chin. It would have to be removed immediately. It was a very long and painful process. Then I had a lengthy shower and washed my hair three times. After all that, I stood naked and studied myself again in the mirror. I looked as if I'd lost at least 2 stone, but that was impossible after such a short time. There was a saggy bit where my stomach used to be. My eyes looked sunken and hollow. But what was worst of all, my genitals seemed to have shrivelled!

Oh God! What I needed was something nice to eat. I hadn't got any cash. Or at least couldn't get to what I had. I saw no immediate signs of replacement credit cards so it would have to be the club. I'd have to walk to St James's.

It was a pleasant day. Pale, wintry sun. I put on one of my better suits which seemed very loose and an overcoat which seemed to weigh a ton. I walked very slowly.

'Your usual, sir?' enquired Bill the barman.

'Just a single please.'

'Goodness, sir, are you not feeling well?'

'No, I've been in hospital.'

'Sorry to hear that, sir. Yes, now you mention it, you do look a bit peaky. Nothing serious, I hope?'

'No, no. I think I've been overworking.'

'Of course, sir. It happens so often these days, doesn't it?'

In the dining room I ordered a Dover sole and a small carafe of Chablis. But when it came, I only managed to finish half the sole and a bit of potato. The Chablis tasted very odd. Walking back to Brook Street was agony. I had appalling indigestion and started sweating profusely. I had to sit down for several minutes on a doorstep somewhere. And when I made it back to my flat, having remembered to switch the phone through from the reception so it rang upstairs, I just took off my jacket and trousers and got into bed and stared at the ceiling. There was a rather nasty little crack across one corner. I'd never noticed it before. I'd have to get the room redecorated... sometime...

After a while I felt very lonely and wondered if there were any messages on the answering service. But there weren't. Gloria must have come in early that morning, written her farewell note to me, taken them all off and incorporated them into this message or whatever it was she'd left on the computer. I'd have to get a temporary secretary to see to it all.

And then the phone rang. Thank goodness not everyone had forgotten me!

'Gregory, it's me, Jane. I'm at the hospital to see you but they say you've been discharged. So I rang your office.'

'Yes, they sort of kicked me out this morning. I think they needed the bed. Can you come along here? It's three hundred, Brook Street.'

'No, I'm awfully sorry, I can't. I was only going to stay half an hour and now I've got something else to do in West London.'

'Oh, I see. Well, tomorrow maybe?'

'Yes, of course. How do you feel?'

'Terrible.'

'Did they tell you what was the matter with you?'

'No. They said they'd send the results of the tests to my GP.'

'Not very satisfactory!'

'No.'

'Well, see you tomorrow. I brought your car back first thing this morning by the way and gave the keys to Gloria.'

'Thanks. I'm awfully grateful. Do you know where she put them?'

'No.'

'Did she say she was leaving?'

'No.'

'Yes, she left me a note – she's gone!'

'Oh dear!' She didn't sound very sorry to hear it.

'Yes. Well, do come any time tomorrow!'

It was getting dark and I was thinking that I might possibly have retrieved my belongings by getting in touch with Lucy's father – my trainer – but it was getting a bit late now. The phone rang again. It was Cristabel.

'I've just rung the hospital and they say you've been discharged!'

'Yes. This morning.'

'Does this mean you're better?'

'No. I think they just wanted the bed!'

'How do you feel?'

'Awful!'

'What are you doing?'

'Lying in bed.'

'I'd better come.'

About half an hour later the entryphone sounded, I let Cristabel in and told her where my bedroom was. She tapped on the door very tentatively and said, 'May I come in?'

She was smiling as she entered, but then she looked at my face and stopped.

'Goodness, they really shouldn't have discharged you. Have you had anything to eat?'

I told her about my visit to the club.

'I'm surprised you made it, the way you look. Would you like a cup of tea?'

'Yes please. The kitchen's off the living room to the right, but there's no milk.'

Cristabel slipped off her overcoat and put it on a chair. She was wearing a tight jumper. God, she was beautiful! I lay there and thought about it while she was away. Soon she reappeared carrying two cups.

'I found some Earl Grey. It's okay without milk... I've been thinking,' she said, sitting down. 'You obviously can't stay here. Where's your secretary by the way?'

'She's left.'

'Very helpful of her!'

'I found a note when I arrived here from the hospital. She said I was impossible!'

'Well, maybe you are, but it seems a bad time to choose to walk out.'

'Yes,' I sighed, 'been with me three years, too!'

'Look, my aunt runs a nursing home in Hampshire. I'll see if she's got room for you. I'm sure you're not hard up, but it's a charity so it won't cost you anything unless you'd like to make a donation when you leave. I'll go and phone her.'

She didn't give me a chance to say no.

'Well that's all arranged,' she said when she came back after a few minutes. 'I'll take you now in my car. It's parked nearby. Do you want any help? You'd better take a few toilet things and pyjamas – and maybe a change of underwear and clothes for when you're allowed up.'

I must have slept most of the way on the back seat. When I woke, the headlights showed we were driving down a very narrow lane.

'Ah, you're awake,' she said, glancing over her shoulder. 'I thought I heard you move. We're nearly there!'

Soon we drove over a cattle grid, into a driveway and drew up in front of a large house. She opened the back door of the car and helped me out.

'Ah, here's Auntie. She's expecting us.'

I looked at the shrouded figure in the shadow of the porch and could hardly believe it. What the hell had I come to? But as the lady welcomed me, I noticed she had kind eyes and a beautiful face, very like Cristabel's.

'Come along in, Gregory. May I call you Gregory? I hear you've not been at all well, but we'll do our best to look after you here. I'll show you to your room. Would you like anything to eat? Supper is over, but we could easily manage an omelette or a boiled egg.'

I said I didn't want anything; just to lie down. I noticed the house was Victorian Gothic as we passed through various gloomy corridors with pitch pine panelling, Auntie leading the way, Cristabel holding me with one arm and carrying my bag in the other.

'Here we are!' said Auntie at last. 'This is you!'

And she showed me into a very pleasant large room.

'And here's your own bathroom. Just sit down and Sister will be along in a few minutes to help you into bed.'

I sank down into the nearest chair. I noticed vaguely that they were all covered in a William Morris fabric.

'Bye, Gregory. See you again soon,' said Cristabel, giving me a bright little wave. 'As Auntie says, you'll be well looked after here.'

They disappeared and within a minute there was a tap on the door and 'Sister' appeared.

'I've come to help you to bed,' she said. She was dressed just like Auntie and my worst fears were confirmed.

'Oh God,' I murmured to myself, 'fucking nuns!!'

4

What happened during the next few months is very hazy in my mind. I must have been very ill and I suppose severely depressed. I now recall various incidents, not necessarily in the correct order. First, and this must have been shortly after I had arrived at the nursing home, I suddenly remembered about my purchase of Toy Boy, my tax affairs and my horses. I became hysterical and tried to get out of bed and get dressed. The doctor was called and he gave me an injection to sedate me. Then Cristabel arrived and said she would take care of everything for me. She came back later with a power of attorney for me to sign in her favour and said that she and the solicitors and accountants would deal with everything and that 'nice Mr Cohen' had agreed to carry on running Toy Boy until I was better and I was not to worry about anything.

Then there was some problem about getting the test results and so I had to be taken to the local hospital and put through the same rigmarole of X-rays, blood tests, etc. all over again. I did keep saying that Dr Smith must have got some test results that he could send to the nursing home but Auntie just patted my arm and said, 'Don't worry, it'll be all right.'

Sometimes I was allowed to get out of bed and sit in an armchair in a dressing gown. The doctor who looked after the patients in the home was apparently also a local GP. I found him very annoying. Every time I asked him if 'they' knew what was the matter with me, he kept replying, 'We'll take you to see the consultant at the hospital when we can get an appointment.'

It seemed like an eternity before I saw the consultant. When I got there he merely looked at my test results, examined me physically and said, 'I think you'll be all right. Just take it easy.'

What was I doing but 'taking it easy'?

When the weather got better, I was allowed to get dressed and walk about in the little garden the nuns had next to their chapel. I remember for the first time in my life watching things slowly coming into bud. I'd never had the time to watch before. And then I remember being terribly excited when the buds on a shrub (I've no idea what it was called) burst into leaf.

'Ah, the new leaf!' I remember saying out loud. But then I remembered that I was supposed to have turned over a different sort of leaf.

'Look where it's got me!' I said to myself over and over. It made me feel unbearably sad as everything sprang into life in the nuns' garden. I became more and more depressed and didn't want to go there any more. I stayed in my room despite Auntie insisting that 'some fresh air would do me good'.

One day, the GP announced that he'd spoken to the consultant again after I'd undergone another lot of tests and, as I didn't seem to be making much progress, they wanted me to see a psychiatrist.

I lay awake that night. 'They think I've gone nuts,' I kept saying to myself.

The psychiatrist was an effete young man, obviously gay. After I had sat down in the chair opposite his desk he spent several minutes reading my file and going, 'Um, um, um,' from time to time. I did wonder why he hadn't bothered to read it before asking me into his room.

'So you've been ill for quite a few months now,' he said at last.

I nodded.

'Tell me, do you have any sexual urges?'

Did he know something about my past, I wondered? 'Not recently,' I replied truthfully.

'Ah! Have you tried masturbating or watching a blue movie, or both?'

'Well, no,' I said, thinking that masturbation might be done under cover, as it were, but I could not really see myself asking Auntie to get me a blue movie to play on the DVD player in my room.

'Maybe you should think about it. You are obviously very depressed. It's difficult to know what to do for the best when someone has had a bad breakdown in their health like you had and is not progressing. You see, all the latest tests have been pretty normal.'

I was glad to hear it, but thought that somebody might have told me so before now.

'But,' the young man was continuing in his languid voice, 'it's probably a case for psychotherapy. If you go back home to London are you able to arrange for someone to look after you? You know, a sort of daily housekeeper?'

I said I hoped I could.

'That's good. I'll refer you to a first class man I know in Harley Street and I'll change your antidepressants to something a little stronger.'

'Excellent!' said Cristabel when I told her about going back to London and the psychotherapy. Apparently at one stage in her life she couldn't paint; went to a psychoanalyst and bingo – she could to paint again!

And so I went back to my flat and office in Brook Street. Cristabel arranged for a Filipino lady, Grace, to come in every day to look after me. She was a good cook and it was lovely to have her around the place, but I have to admit I missed Auntie and her nuns. I'd become rather institutionalised and grown used to their seemingly unconditional kindness. Auntie seemed pleased with the cheque I gave her when I left.

I needed a routine. I wasn't ready to start work again but, now I was home, I desperately wanted to start back on the road to normality, and I was hoping the sessions with the psychoanalyst would help to bring about my recovery.

So now we get to Dr Greenbaum. I remember my first session with him very well. His room was almost unfurnished. It had a couch, an armchair for him, and a hard one for me at the initial interview, a table and a table lamp. But no pictures and no curtains, only a blind always half drawn down. Dr G was of indeterminate age; always sombrely dressed in a dark grey suit, white shirt and plain tie. His accent was curious. Where did he come from originally? Germany? South America? He had a very large hooked nose and thick spectacles.

'Do please zit down, Mr Bannister,' he said, indicating the hard chair. 'I have had a report about you from my colleague. I vill do my best to help. Zese things often take zome time. I have zis vacancy every day Monday to Friday at eleven o'clock. Most people find it helpful to lie on ze couch. Just zay vot comes into your mind and tell me also about any dreams you may have.'

I duly lay on the couch. It was dead flat with a small cushion under my head, and a paper towel over the cushion. All rather uncomfortable, I thought. I shuffled about a bit and then supposed I ought to say something.

'I fainted when I went into a church and I've felt ill every since. But I expect you know all that from the reports you've had. And I think I've got this terrible hang-up about women. I've thought about it a lot since I've been ill. I'm like a dog at a lamp post when I see a pretty woman. I think it's to do with my mother, you see. She did what my father always used to refer to as "a bunk" when I was three.'

I hoped this might elicit a response like, 'I see,' or something similar. But there was silence. So I went on, 'I always wanted her to come back but she didn't. She just sometimes sent me presents like this ring I've brought to show you. It has an inscription from her inside it, "To G love from Mum". Would you like to see it?'

I waved it towards Dr Greenbaum behind me. He appeared to ignore it and when I turned round to look at him, he seemed to be staring straight through me. Eventually I became embarrassed; lay down again and put the ring on my little finger.

'Then I had a nanny. I hated her. She was fat, had hairy legs and a very loud voice. She was always telling me off. One of her favourite expressions was, "Gregory, you've got to turn over a new leaf." So that was what came into my mind when I first felt ill and went to Dr Smith and he told me I might become seriously ill if I didn't change my lifestyle. Have you had a report from him? But now I'm told my illness is maybe not physical but psychological. It seems unfair. I tried to turn over a new leaf and immediately for the first time in my life I've become really ill. I wish I could go back to how I was before, but I know I can't. I feel too depressed to do anything. I've been given these new antidepressants and told not to drive, not to drink, and not to work. I think all that those previous antidepressants have done is made me impotent – and that's even more depressing, of course. But you know most of this from those reports you've had. I'd better tell you about my childhood. At first, I went to a day prep school in London. I think Dad wanted me at home for company. He always used to call me "old chap" and we went away for very nice holidays in Scotland and Cornwall and places like that. He didn't really like foreigners.'

Then I realised that this perhaps wasn't a very tactful remark. So as to cover up for this, I continued brightly, 'Of course I have would have been delighted to go to the Continent myself, but he didn't want it. Nanny didn't ever come with us on these holidays, thank God. She went to stay with her sister in Wales. Then my aunt – that's my father's sister – suggested I should be sent away to boarding school. I hated the idea. My father, I think, also hated my going away. At the beginning of term I was always sick before the day I had to catch the train. I suppose I hoped it would mean I didn't have to go, but Dad always insisted. He used to drive me to the station. Secretly, I thought he looked a bit green himself as we waited on the platform for the school train to come into the station. And then at the last minute he would take out his wallet, thrust a tenner into my left hand, and shake me firmly by the right and say, "Have a good term, old chap," and then turn on his heel and walk away. Back to the office I suppose. He was a property dealer and developer by the way, like me. I took over what was left of his business after it was more or less ruined by Lola. But I'll come on to her later. I'm sorry if this is a bit rambling. I hope you can follow?'

Silence – Oh well! Just carry on, I thought. I suppose it's good 'therapy' just getting all this off my chest.

'Well, as I said, I think if I'd had a nice kind mother at home it would have all have been all right and I wouldn't have developed what my aunt called "bad ways" when I got away to school. I got expelled three times, you know. On the first occasion my father sent a telegram to Mother – "Gregory expelled and at home. Please come." He showed it to me before he sent it off. But she didn't come. All she did was to phone and take me out to tea at Claridge's and tell me I'd been a very, very naughty boy. But I could tell even at age thirteen that she didn't really mean it! She was secretly amused. She sat there in a very smart suit and hat picking at a piece of cake and sipping her Lapsang Suchong. And then she put a cigarette into her holder and lit it. She was a most beautiful woman; slim and dark with a very pretty face, and long black hair and eyelashes. She'd run off with a French businessman and they lived in Paris. She always referred to him as "the Count", but my father said it was a lot of nonsense and he wasn't really a Count. As far as I know they never got married. She died when I was twenty-two. I think I only saw her twice more after the tea at Claridge's. It was probably after each time I was expelled. The first expulsion, by the way, was for being found drunk with two other boys after dark in the school grounds. After that, my father managed to get me into one of the London day schools. But that didn't last very long. I was found smoking in the changing rooms. Breach of school rules. So then my father managed to get me into a liberal co-ed boarding school in Scotland where the rules weren't half as strict. That's where I discovered that I liked girls very much, even though I was only fifteen.'

I stopped there and hoped for some reaction to this revelation. But there was still silence.

'Are you going to say anything?' I asked.

'I'm just listening carefully to vot you are telling me.'

Oh good, I thought. Well, at least that was something. I continued, 'I think I'd better tell you in detail about when I fainted. It was connected with this very beautiful artist friend I have called Cristabel. I haven't slept with her. She's very strict. She's a Catholic.'

And I started telling Dr Greenbaum exactly what had happened. But after a few words, he interrupted me.

'I zink you are afraid of zumthing. But we must stop for today. Ze time is up!'

As I emerged into Harley Street, I thought it was not much advice for the £70 that Dr Greenbaum was apparently going to charge each time he saw me.

After that memorable first session, I can't, of course, remember in detail what was said every day that I went to see him, but certain conversations stand out. It was some time later when I told him, 'I'm thinking about Jasper, Jasper Cohen. He's a hard sod, but he agreed to carry on running this company that I bought from him while I'm not well. He didn't need to do that.'

'Maybe you project your own hard bits into Jasper?'

'I don't understand!'

'You, yourself, may be hard, but you don't like to zee yourself as such. Zo you get rid of it by putting it into Jasper!'

'But Jasper is hard!'

'Ve always project vere ze cap fits.'

'But that's mad. Jasper is a mean sod.'

'Very vell. If you don't agree viz vot I say, it is up to you!'

This produced a lengthy and resentful silence from me. It sounded totally barmy, like when some weeks before Dr Greenbaum had said he did not 'zink' my problems were anything to do with my mother. I did begin to wonder! Clocking up the hours – not even full hours, only fifty minutes I discovered – at £70 per hour. Well, at least I don't have far to go. He was at the south end of Harley Street – most of these analysts are found in Hampstead apparently because that was where Freud had lived.

And then I remember telling Dr G one day about the sort of life I was leading and how boring it was: 'But you must know, Dr Greenbaum, I lead a very reclusive life. When I first came back to London I had somebody to come in every day to get my meals and look after me. But after a couple of weeks I came to the conclusion I could manage on my own. So I get up at eight o'clock and listen to the news on the radio while I have some orange juice, coffee and a roll. I get the rolls from the bakers down the road. Then I have a shave and a shower and get dressed and read the paper for a bit. Then it's time to come and see you. It's lucky you're not far away. Then after I leave you I stop off at a little café I know on the way back to Brook Street and have lunch and a very small glass of wine. Then I have a sleep. I don't usually sleep for very long and sometimes I lie awake and think about what we've talked about in the session, but more likely about one of my ex-girlfriends. I then get up and have a cup of tea and read a book for about an hour or so. Something light. I'm getting through an awful lot of Agatha Christies! Nobody ever seems to phone me and I never get any post. I think Cristabel and the doctor have arranged something so that it all goes to my lawyers. At six o'clock every evening I ring Cristabel because she finishes painting then. We have a chat. Then I go to my club and have dinner. Only one glass of wine again and a cup of coffee in the Reading Room. By the way, as you know I was told not to drink while taking these antidepressants, but I've read the instructions enclosed with them and it says only "avoid" alcohol, so that's what I'm trying to do. Then I walk home and go to bed. I don't feel very well most of the time and I often wonder if there's something still physically wrong with me that tests didn't reveal. At the weekend I go and see Cristabel after lunch on Saturday, I stay on her sofa Saturday night and I'm with her all day Sunday. I don't go to church with her. I'm afraid I might faint again. She's very kind to me, but very strict. She cooks me nice meals and often we go to an art gallery together. Sometimes she lets me watch while she paints. I don't think I really understand her paintings, which are abstracts by the way, even though I bought two of them for my reception area, which is how I got to know her. She's very beautiful. She has lovely breasts and long, dark brown hair. Her face is exquisite. But she never lets me touch her. She says our friendship is "not like that". It's all rather odd, don't you think? I can't make out where she's "coming from", if you know what I mean.'

There was the usual silence. Then Dr Greenbaum said, 'I zink you are telling me that you have my breast from Monday to Friday and Cristabel's on Saturday and Sunday. You need ze food, but it is food for ze mind and ze soul – intangible!'

Occasionally, very occasionally, Dr Greenbaum will ask me a few questions like, 'Do you never listen to ze music?'

'No, I think I'm tone deaf.'

'Have you no close friends?'

'No, I suppose not. I was very close to my father and worked with him until he died. I have or did have lots of business acquaintances – but they are only acquaintances. And as you know I've had rather a lot of girlfriends. But none of them have lasted for any length of time. I suppose I'm quite friendly with the three trainers I have my horses with. But that's really friendship on a professional basis. They're a very long way away and seem to be only interested in horses!'

'Like you ver only interested in business and girls!'

And then after one weekend, 'Dr Greenbaum, I feel terrible today. I suppose because it's a Monday and I couldn't see Cristabel at the weekend. She'd gone to see her aunt at that nursing home I told you about. But I didn't want to go there again! So I went for a walk in Regent's Park on Saturday and saw some of the animals in the zoo. They are nice to look at but don't smell too good. Then on Sunday I had a long walk in Hyde Park. I like Hyde Park very much. My club is closed on a Sunday so I tried to cook myself a meal on Sunday evening. I went to a supermarket and got... but you don't want to hear about my cooking. Maybe it was eating what I'd cooked that has made me feel so ill!'

'I zink it was because you ver missing Cristabel and missing me, of course!'

'You keep on about my missing you, but I'm only coming to see you to try and get better, not because I like you particularly, Dr Greenbaum! What I want you to tell me is why I fainted in church. But we never seem to get on to that.'

There was a long silence.

'Well, go on, say something!' I felt my anger rising.

'I zink you see me now, zis morning, as the bad breast.'

'Oh what a lot of rubbish! I'm just pissed off because I had a bad weekend!'

Dr Greenbaum remained silent for the rest of the session.

While I was having my lunch (and I had two glasses of wine with it) I did think maybe I'd hurt his feelings. But then, I decided, he deserved it.

When I telephoned Cristabel that evening I told her I was going to stop seeing Dr Greenbaum because it was all taking too long. I felt I wasn't getting anywhere. I said that I had heard about something called cognitive behavioural therapy that people said was very good and gave quick results. She was very frosty indeed. She reminded me that the psychiatrist had suggested that I went to Dr Greenbaum as he was a very well-known analyst – I was lucky to have got a vacancy with him. There was no quick fix for my problem. She knew I felt too ill to work and perhaps, she thought, it was the guilt I was eventually feeling for 'the life I had led'. This last phrase was uttered with great emphasis! And if I packed up going to analysis, which had helped her greatly in the past, she wouldn't speak to me again...

After I had digested this tirade I thought firstly, that possibly I felt more ill than ever and secondly, that I couldn't do without Cristabel. So I went back meekly to see Dr. Greenbaum the next day.

'Look, Dr Greenbaum, I'm sorry I was angry yesterday but we don't seem to be making any progress in curing my illness. You keep telling me about good and bad breasts and projections, but I feel just as ill as when I first came to see you. Why don't we discuss why I fainted?'

'You can tell me vot you think if you vish.'

'I don't know!' I almost shouted. 'That's what I want you to tell *me*.'

'I can only follow your associations and interpret them for you. I am not a magician! By the way, do you never have any dreams?'

'Lots. But I can never remember them.'

'If you try to remember them, maybe it would help!'

And so there was silence between us. What on earth was he doing while I lay there silently? Did he have a small book in his lap which he secretly read? When the session was over I turned round quickly and looked at him, but there was no book. He sat there with his hands on the arms of his chair and then merely inclined his head by way of goodbye.

But one day I tried asking Dr Greenbaum a question and much to my surprise, he gave me an answer.

'Dr Greenbaum, why do you think it is that I've repeated this pattern of being obsessed by a woman and then growing tired of her?'

'I zink you idealise them, particularly their physical attributes, zen when you discover they are just human beings like the rest of us, you are disappointed. You idealise your friend Cristabel at the moment and zis is perpetuated because she does not let you touch her and zo she remains the ideal object you zee.'

I thought about this for a few minutes.

'That could easily be true, Dr Greenbaum. Thank you very much.'

And I thought a great deal about it afterwards. At last, we seemed to be making some progress.

And then after about four months of seeing Dr Greenbaum Monday to Friday, one morning in the middle of July he announced he would give me his holiday dates. I was amazed. It hadn't occurred to me that psychoanalysts took holidays when they were in the middle of treating a patient.

'I vill be away for approximately four weeks from ze fourth August to ze end of ze month. Would you like to make a note of zat please?'

'But what am I to do while you are away?'

'Ah, you vill be missing me at last!'

'Well not so much missing you as needing you! But look, when doctors or lawyers go on holiday they have an assistant or someone to take their place. Are you just going to leave me?'

'Zat is vot happens. It is often very good for ze patient!'

Bloody hell! I phoned Cristabel.

'Dr Greenbaum is going on holiday. Did your analyst chap do that?'

'Well it was a lady actually, but yes, they do take holidays.'

'But what am I to do? He'll be away from the fourth of August till the end of the month! I mean, what shall I do all day?'

There was a short silence.

'Mummy and I are going to the South of France on the tenth of August for three weeks. Perhaps you'd like to come with us?'

5

I see myself sitting opposite Cristabel's mother in the hotel in Aix-en-Provence. It's the first evening of the holiday and so far she has scarcely uttered a word. She's still clad in a black tent-like dress and dark glasses which she had on when we all met at Heathrow. The three of us are finishing dinner. Cristabel has chattered ceaselessly to make up for her mother's silence. But now her mother has just taken off her dark glasses for the first time and I notice she has a very beautiful thin face and the same eyes as Cristabel and Auntie, but there are dark rings under them; she's obviously been crying. She blinks and smiles at me.

'Yes, I know, I look terrible. I'm sorry. And I'm sorry that I've hardly said a word since we met. Has Cristabel told you that my husband has just left me?'

'Er... well, she did mention it...' I said.

'Yes, he's gone off with a girl aged twenty. New model, you see. I'm getting past it!'

'Don't be so silly, Mummy,' said Cristabel.

'I'll talk more in the morning. Call me Jessica, by the way. But now I think I'd like to go to bed. I mustn't have any coffee otherwise I shan't sleep... will you excuse me please, Gregory?'

Cristabel said she wanted to smoke so we went into the garden.

'I feel a bit guilty about bringing you here with Mummy like this. I've given her a pep talk and told her she must try and cheer up. After all, my father went off once before but came back after about four weeks!'

'How long ago did he leave?' I asked.

'Last week. But it's been a bit "iffy" for some time. I suppose that was why he said he didn't want to come on this holiday. Although Mummy and he often do things separately.'

'Are your father and mother both Catholics?'

'Yes, but Daddy doesn't take it very seriously!'

'I don't understand,' I said, 'your mother is obviously very beautiful, what little I've seen of her in that tent-like black dress.'

'Oh yes, she is. She's only just fifty. She had me when she was twenty. We're often taken for sisters.'

Cristabel shook her head sadly. She stood there silhouetted against the illuminated water of the swimming pool. She looked absolutely lovely.

'Well, don't feel too sad about your mother,' I said, leaning forward to kiss her.

'No!' she said, putting her hand firmly on my chest. 'You know what I've said before, we're just friends.'

'But I was only trying to comfort you…'

'You've come here for rest and quiet, and you mustn't get over-excited.' She was looking very stern. 'By the way, I'm worried about Mummy drinking too much and I noticed *you* had three glasses of wine at dinner.'

'Ah yes, well actually I've stopped taking those awful antidepressant tablets and so I can drink a bit again.'

She drew in her breath and then ferociously blew out some cigarette smoke, incidentally showing off her magnificent bosom.

'Are you really sure that's wise?' she said. 'Stopping the medication? Oh dear, oh dear!... Anyhow, I'll see you in the morning. I'd better go and see if Mummy's all right.'

Well, I thought, I suppose this is going to be a *bit* better than being on my own in stuffy Central London in the heat of August.

Jessica didn't appear at breakfast the following morning. Cristabel did join me and announced she wanted to walk into the town before it became too hot, but I needn't come if I didn't want to.

It was a beautiful hotel with a lovely garden and pool and it had all that I wanted at that moment. Even so, I would have liked to have gone with Cristabel but I knew she always walked very quickly. I was frightened that I might feel faint in the heat. Fainting was something that I was still very afraid of.

'Thanks, maybe tomorrow or the next day,' I said. 'It feels a bit strange at the moment – you know, after my routine of living on my own, just seeing Dr G and going to the club to have dinner every day.'

So I took a copy of *Le Figaro* and went and sat on a lounger by the pool. A waiter came and gave me a towel to lie on even though I was dressed in shirt and trousers. Having the towel made me think I might take a swim later, but for the moment I tried to read *Le Figaro*. But I always find it very tiring reading French and after a while I just lay back and enjoyed the sun. It was a Monday and probably for that reason, there was nobody else around. I must have dozed off because I was woken by a splash and a lady in one of those petalled bathing caps was swimming in the pool. She swam quietly up and down several times and then slowly emerged up the pool steps nearest to where I lay. Goodness, she had a wonderful figure. It was just like Venus rising from the sea. And then she peeled off her bathing cap and shook her hair out – and I realised it was Jessica!

'Good God, and her husband's left her!' I thought, and then I waved.

'Oh, hello,' she said casually. 'I didn't realise it was you.'

She went and fetched her towel and started very decorously to dry herself, perched on the lounger beside me.

'May I come and sit over here with you?'

'Of course, I'd be delighted!'

She went and fetched her things from the other side of the pool. I hadn't noticed her smoking before, but now she groped in her handbag and lit a cigarette. It obviously ran in the family.

'I'm so sorry to be so antisocial.'

'Well, it's understandable.'

'But, you've been ill – very ill. Cristabel explained it all when she said she'd invited you and I was looking forward to meeting you. I said I'd try to cheer you up. And look what a wet blanket I've been so far!'

'Cristabel seems to think her father will come back.'

'I'm not sure that I want him back. I feel rejected, you see. If he wants this girl he'd better have her. She's one of his students, of course!'

'Oh, I see, he teaches.'

'Ah yes. University. English. I think these young girls nowadays just think it's a game trying to get their tutor to sleep with them.'

She chattered on about nothing in particular and in due course lit another cigarette from the stub of the first, ground the stub furiously on the pavement to extinguish it, and then threw it into the bushes nearby. Her face was a picture of ill-suppressed rage.

'I suppose it's too early for a drink?' she said.

'Well, it's only eleven, but I'll call the waiter if you like.'

'No, better wait until after twelve for alcohol. But shall we go on the terrace and have a coffee?'

'Of course!'

'But first I must change out of this wet swimsuit.'

I ordered two large espressos, as agreed, and waited on

the terrace. Jessica soon reappeared clad in a low-cut white blouse and tight blue jeans. I wondered vaguely if this was for my benefit.

'Well, let's forget my troubles,' she said. 'There's nothing I can do except put up with it. Tell me, what happened to you? Cristabel was rather vague. She said she knew you because you'd bought two of her paintings for your office.'

'Yes, I think they're very good, and a lot of people have admired them. But I don't really understand them. Cristabel has been very, very kind to me. It started with me ringing her bell very late one night. It was freezing cold – snowing – and I was just in my shirt and trousers with no money, no keys, no credit cards, no phone… '

Jessica raised her eyebrows and said, 'I wonder she let you in. She's awfully puritanical. But you must know that by now.'

'Yes. Well, I've spent practically every weekend with her since I came out of your sister's nursing home. Cristabel told you, no doubt, about my fainting in church with her and then going into the nursing home?'

'Yes, she told me that, but I didn't realise that you'd stayed with her every weekend.'

'You mustn't get the wrong idea. I think Cristabel's stunning, but she never once let me touch her.'

Jessica actually threw back her head and laughed. 'How typical of her, and how very frustrating for you!!'

'Yes, very. In fact, it's nearly driven me mad.'

She put her hand over mine. 'I think you need a drink now. Come on, shall we have a *pastis*?'

We had one, then another.

'Do you know why you fainted in the church?' she asked.

'No idea, really. Perhaps I'm frightened of churches or maybe God – except I don't believe in Him.'

'Sometimes I wonder if I do. Particularly at the moment! But come on, I've got to try and cheer you up. You may not believe this, having seen me in my black tent of yesterday, but I'm a dress designer. Not *haute couture*, more high street.'

I found Jessica very easy to talk to and eventually asked her if Cristabel had always been so aloof.

'No. She's an only child. Until she was about seventeen or eighteen she was quite what you might say "normal", then she suddenly became fiercely religious. I suppose that's the right way of putting it. She said she wanted to go to art college and not university and has been what I can only describe as "self-contained" ever since. And she has been quite successful as an artist. Her father and I thought we should have to support her but she manages on her own!'

Then Jessica told me some very funny stories about the fashion world and we were laughing a great deal when Cristabel arrived back.

'Goodness, it's hot in the town,' she said rather grumpily, and sat down looking disapprovingly at our almost empty glasses of *pastis*. 'Well, you two seem to be getting on well together!'

'Yes, darling, Gregory has been telling me how very kind you've been to him. Shall we order some lunch?'

'No, I don't think I want anything. I feel so hot. I had a coffee and one of those almond croissant things in the town. I think I'll have a cold shower and lie down.'

When she'd gone, 'Mmm, a bit huffy don't you think?' said Jessica, smiling conspiratorially. 'Shall you and me have something to eat on our own then?'

Did she actually flutter her eyelashes at me, or was it my imagination? The lunch was the sort of thing only the French can manage, light and delicious, rounded off with strawberries and cream. And for the first time in months I was feeling relaxed when one of the waiters came up to me and said, 'Monsieur Bannister, telephone.'

'Damn! Who the hell can it be?' I muttered to Jessica. 'Nobody knows I'm here.'

'Hello,' I growled angrily into the instrument. 'Gregory Bannister. Who is it?'

'Greg!' said a familiar voice. 'I asked for Cristabel. What are you doing in France? It's George.'

'Why did the waiter bring the phone to me, then?'

'Well, it's these Frogs, isn't it? Don't understand plain English. I said I wanted to speak to Miss Ashton and they said they thought she was in her room and didn't want to be disturbed, but what was it about before they tried her. And I said it was about Gregory Bannister, so they gave you the phone. I phoned the hotel because, as you must know, Cristabel doesn't ever switch on her mobile. It's for emergencies only. Well, anyhow, you must be feeling better!'

'I am, a bit. Thanks. Yes, I'm with Cristabel and her mother. They invited me to come here with them. But what did you want to say to Cristabel about me?'

'Well, if you're feeling better, I suppose I can tell you as you'll have to know sooner or later anyhow. Look, brace yourself. The bank's calling in that extra loan you took out for the stock. I think it's for half a million, isn't it? They say it was only for six months and you should be reducing it and the interest is mounting, etc. etc. etc. You said you'd be disposing of some of Toy Boy's assets almost immediately. But as far as they know, nothing's been sold.'

I felt my jaw muscles tightening. 'But I've been ill!' I almost shouted.

'Yes, look, I know all about it. Your doctor spoke to me and the bank. Your friend Cristabel has been most attentive and helpful. She has your power of attorney. But there's been two increases in interest rates since the spring. And well, you know what mean sods these banks can be!'

'I'll fly back at once,' I said. 'Make an appointment for me to see the bank manager for the day after tomorrow – that's Wednesday – please.'

'You're sure you'll be okay?'

'Yes, yes.'

'You will gather that most unfortunately I have to leave you...' I said to Jessica.

'What a shame,' she said, putting her hand over mine again, 'just as we were getting on so well! Are you sure you're going to be all right?'

'I shall have to be. Only I can sort out this problem. My bank has called in a half million pound loan.'

'But can't Cristabel deal with it somehow?'

I was in the middle of packing when Cristabel knocked and came into my room.

'Gregory, you simply cannot go back to London on your own and try and sort this loan thing out.'

I knew this would be coming and said nothing; merely went on packing.

'Gregory, are you listening! Stop packing at once!'

'Nobody but me can sort this out.'

'Leave it to me and the solicitors.'

'No, I must do it myself.'

'Gregory, please don't be so silly.'

She grasped my wrists to stop me putting anything else in the suitcase. But I'd made up my mind.

'I'm going,' I said, rather roughly disengaging myself.

She looked at me furiously.

'Well, I wash my hands of you if you're going to be so stupid after all I've done to help you.'

I think I said something silly in reply like, 'Okay Miss Pontia Pilate,' but I've tried to erase it from my memory.

I reflect now that making bold statements about doing things and actually doing them are different matters.

On the plane back to London my resolve began to drain away, to be replaced by what I can only describe as a feeling of emptiness in my guts. I had always, and I suppose had got this from my father, tried to approach difficult business meetings with a feeling of determination and confidence. But not this time. I had a sense of foreboding and by the time I got back to Brook Street, I was wishing to God that I'd left it all to Cristabel and the solicitors. But it would have been a terrible loss of face not to go on now.

So on Wednesday morning, having taken not one but two of my anti-anxiety pills, I was sitting opposite a stoney-faced bank manager. He was not the one I'd been used to dealing with in the past. The new one was youngish, Scottish, and in a tight black pinstriped three-piece suit. He was very carefully groomed from his short ginger but greying hair down to the neatly-clipped fingernails that he drummed on the top of my file, which lay open in front of him.

'I don't understand your attitude,' I said. 'You know I've been ill.'

'I sympathise.' (He didn't sound very sympathetic.) 'It's the extra loan for the stock we're particularly concerned about at the moment, although your indebtedness to the bank was very considerable before that. In fact, I can't understand how my predecessor allowed your overall indebtedness to the bank to reach the level it has. The terms for the extra loan were that stock was to be sold as soon as possible and the loan paid off in any event within six months! I think maybe you should get someone to look after your affairs.'

'But I did. I appointed Miss Ashton as my attorney and she arranged for Mr Cohen, from whom I bought the company, to continue running it while I was indisposed.'

McGinger (as I had already christened him in my mind) flicked over a few papers in my file.

'Mr Cohen? We haven't heard from him as far as I can see.'

He fixed me with a cold stare.

'Well, when do you want the loan repaid by? It's five hundred thousand isn't it?' I said weakly.

'Five hundred and fifteen thousand, three hundred and twenty one, as of today, including the interest. Within twenty-one days please.'

'Suppose I can't repay within that time?'

'We have a charge on the assets of your company and your personal guarantee. I don't think I have to spell it out to you, Mr Bannister. Perhaps you can find an alternative financial institution willing to help you.'

I tried for a final time.

'But – but... I've been banking with you for years. Is this the way to treat me now, when I've been unwell and unable to run my business?'

'You must understand it's the risk to us, Mr Bannister. Please don't blame me personally. It's orders from Head Office. Those were the terms of the loan.'

At first I felt angry, then I felt sick.

'The bastard's after me!' I kept saying to myself. If I didn't pay off everything I owed to the bank quickly he would try to make me bankrupt. I could see that fanatical gleam in his eyes.

I didn't take a taxi. I walked very slowly from Oxford Street, where my bank was, towards Brook Street. Although it was early in the morning, it was already getting very warm. I came to a pub in a side street. It had chairs and tables on the pavement outside but there were no customers yet. I sat down at one of the tables and took my jacket off as I was dripping with sweat. All those things to be done to avoid bankruptcy! But was I capable of doing them? So many things to do and so much money to repay; I felt like crying. In the state I was, it felt like having to climb Mount Everest.

Looking back, from then on, I felt as though I was being swept along and in danger of drowning in some awful fast-flowing river.

The sequence of events is rather jumbled in my mind. When I arrived back at Brook Street I didn't go up to my

flat but sat down at the desk in my office. It was dusty.
Why the hell had it not been dusted? I'd been paying the
cleaners whilst I was away. I felt like smashing its glass top
but instead I put my head in my hands. What was I to do?
I could refinance, but that would be at a very high rate of
interest. Or I could sell the stock quickly... But what the hell
had Jasper been doing, or not doing? I phoned him.

'Greg! Long time no hear. Are you better?'

'No, not completely. But look Jasper, I'm in trouble. My
bank has called in the extra loan – the half a million I had to
take out to pay for those bloody teddies I wasn't expecting to
have to buy. Have you sold them?'

There was a silence. 'Well, no.'

'Have you tried!!?'

'No. Now listen, Greg. All I was asked to do was to keep the
company running and that's exactly what I've done. You'll find
there's a good trading profit. But I was never told specifically
to run down the stock. I expect we've sold a few of the teddies
in the normal course of business, but that's all! My boy, I'm
sorry you're in trouble. I'd offer to help myself if I could, but
all my cash is tied up at the moment. Anyhow, we must talk
sometime about the company. I don't want to go on running
it for ever and there's the question of the management fee.'

'Okay, okay Jasper, we'll talk. But let me refinance this
loan first. I've only got twenty-one days. You know anyone?'

'Sure! But they'll charge you!'

Still, it would only be until I could sell those bloody bears
and some of the rest of the stock...

Later I considered the possibility of liquidating some of my
assets to pay down the loan. The only trouble was I hadn't
got many assets and only twenty-one days to realise them. I
had six racehorses, an Aston Martin, my share portfolio, my
office and flat – and that was about it.

I started with my stockbroker.

'Ah, Greg, nice to hear from you. You've been unwell, I gather. I had a letter from a lady – your attorney. Do not disturb, etc... '

I cut him short.

'I need some money quickly. I can't remember exactly what I've got with you.'

'How much do you want?'

'About five hundred and fifteen thousand pounds.'

'Phew! Well the market hasn't been too good this year, to say the least, and it is very low at the moment. Let me get you up on the screen... Ah yes, you sold a block of M&S didn't you to buy the new Aston Martin, and then another big block of Tesco to buy two more racehorses at the end of last year. I'm afraid you're down to just under £450,000 at today's prices. Don't think there'll be any capital gains tax. What do you want me to do?'

'Sell everything! That may keep the bank quiet while I forage around for the rest.'

'Okay, if you must. Will do. Remember there'll be charges to be deducted. I hope you feel better soon.'

'Thanks. I will if I can sort this lot out!'

My next call was to the car dealer.

'Look, I've been ill and been told not to drive at the moment. How much would I get for the Aston?'

'Mmm. I'm sorry you're not well Mr. Bannister. Newish, isn't it?'

'Yes, last October.'

'Ah ha! I remember it now.'

'The market's very quiet. I'm afraid I couldn't give you more than £85,000.'

'But, bloody hell, I paid over £110,000 for it!'

'I know, and low mileage no doubt. But that's the market, I'm afraid. If you want me to try for more I can put it into an auction for you, or of course you could try a private sale by advertising.'

'Thanks, I'll think about it.'

After that I forgot about trying to sell the horses quickly. I phoned the bank and told them I'd pay them about £450,000 as soon as the money came through from my stockbrokers and asked if they would roll over the rest of the loan until I had sold off some of the stock, which I hoped to do very quickly.

They agreed, but the bloodsuckers said they'd charge me an extra three per cent!

That was on Friday. On Saturday morning, I received a letter. I can remember the wording almost exactly:

> As agreed on the phone the bank is pleased to assist you by accepting your terms for paying down the extra loan for the stock of Toy Boy Limited, but with an increase in the rate of interest by three per cent until that loan is paid off in full. I look forward to the remittance from your stockbrokers with whom I have been in telephonic communication. However, as I indicated at our recent meeting, we are concerned at your overall level of indebtedness to the bank. Without the extra loan for the stock, but including interest as at today's date, this now stands at £2.85 million.
>
> I am concerned also that you are overdrawn £10,000 on your personal current account. I know you have been unwell but now that you are back in London, I hope you can put forward a sensible timetable for paying off these amounts within a reasonable timeframe.

After I had read the letter I just went and lay on my bed. I was now totally convinced that McGinger was after me.

On Monday morning, I phoned the office cleaning contractors and took out my general rage on them.

When I had calmed down, a voice in my head kept telling

me I would feel better if I made a start on trying to sort it all out.

So I went to see Jasper.

'Well, I've got the bank off my back for the time being,' I said to him.

'Good, and you're not looking too bad. But you've lost weight, my boy!'

'I know. Probably a good thing!'

Then we looked through the books of Toy Boy together. There was an operating profit of nearly £50,000 since I bought the shares.

'As we're friends, what I'm going to suggest, Greg, is that I take the £50,000 as a management fee. It's less than I'd usually charge, but that will put you exactly on the same footing as if you'd just bought the company, wouldn't it?'

What could I say?

'Horace has done a good job. Kept him from other things I had lined up for him. You might like to send him a little thank you!'

I thought it seemed a little rich on top of the £50,000, but said nothing.

'Are you going to be able to cope?'

'I shall have to!'

'By the way, what's happened to that lovely friend of yours, Cristabel? She came to see me once. A real cracker.'

'She's still in France at the moment.'

'Bad luck... well anyhow, I'll leave it all to you now. I'll tell Horace to move out of his room at Toy Boy's head office tomorrow.'

I think my next stop was my solicitors.

I told George how I had managed to keep the bank quiet and the various things I had to do now so that I could give a timetable to the bank manager, who was harassing me.

First, make the staff of Toy Boy redundant and close the office, warehouse and shops.

Second, sell the office, warehouse and shops.

Third, sell the stock, including the teddy bears, as soon as possible.

I told him I couldn't deal with everything myself. I was feeling better but I wasn't fully recovered. If I dealt with the sale of the properties, could his firm please arrange the staff redundancies and an auction sale for all the stock? An auction seemed to me to be the only way of getting the money in quickly. A 'closing down' sale wouldn't do. It would drag on for ages and I would still have some stock left at the end of it.

George sucked in his fat cheeks. 'Well, we've got a lot of staff on holiday at the moment as it's August, but we'll see what we can do. I'd like to help you, Greg. You'd better work out exactly what you want and let me know and then we'll cost it out per hour.'

I was so pleased that George was prepared to help that I almost felt like hugging the great, fat bugger! I went home feeling much happier and had the best night's sleep since returning to London.

6

I was puzzled by my personal account being overdrawn. I had left all that sort of thing to Gloria and my accountants. And I didn't seem to have had a tax demand for some time, which was very odd. Normally they rained down like confetti! I phoned my accountants.

'Hello Greg!' This wasn't the partner I normally dealt with, Wally – he was on holiday. This was his partner, Jim. 'Wally told me you weren't well and shouldn't be disturbed. He said before he went on holiday that he was writing to that lady friend of yours.'

'Well, she's away in France. What was it about?'

'We've had a nasty letter. HMRC want to investigate you.'

'Why, for heaven's sake?'

'Well, I can't quite remember offhand.'

'Is it serious?'

'I don't know. Hang on a minute and I'll get your file.'

There was quite a lengthy pause and a lot of rustling of papers, then, 'They say you owe them just over a million in tax!'

I thought I was going to faint. I was sitting at the desk in my office. The desk seemed to go up and down as if it were in a ship in a rough sea. I pressed the palms of my hands on it and tried to keep calm.

'You'd better send me a copy of this letter you sent to Miss

Ashton. For God's sake, do I really owe them over a million? And if so, when do they want it?'

'Greg, I don't know if it's right or wrong and they don't give a deadline. But if the claim is correct they'll probably want an interim payment forthwith. That's the usual sort of thing. You know how fierce they can be!'

'Would you please just fax a copy of the letter to my office straight away!'

After I'd rung off, I sat back in my chair, put my head in my hands and said, 'Oh God, what next?' I felt totally numb. Almost for something to do, I ordered a temporary secretary from an agency. She was called Ann; plain, middle-aged and with a sagging bosom, but she was efficient and someone to talk to. She printed out everything on the computer and I read it through. Most of it seemed like ancient history.

Then I took a very deep breath and asked her if she would please show me how to work the computer myself.

Lying in bed that night I understood what had been happening to all my post and telephone messages. Presumably Cristabel had been dealing with them all; I had never thought to ask her. That is the sort of thing that happens when you are depressed. I tried phoning the hotel in Aix but gathered that Cristabel and her mother had checked out!

The letter from HMRC was very terse and lacking in detail. It made me so agitated that I simply couldn't wait for Wally to return from his holiday and I made an appointment to see someone at the Tax Office in Holborn myself to try and get more information.

From the outside it was a most dismal building, probably dating from the early 1950s, rebuilt after war time bomb damage. Its metal-framed windows and post-war brickwork would have depressed anyone. Inside, it looked as if the cream-coloured walls hadn't been painted since it was built. I sat on a hard chair in a minute windowless waiting room for some time before I was summoned. It was a bit like waiting to see the dentist.

'Come in please, Mr Bannister, and sit down.'

The official was surprisingly young and very dishevelled. His tie was askew, his hair long and greasy and one of his jacket buttons was hanging by a thread. He pushed his hair out of his eyes and fixed me with the sort of gaze that hadn't come my way since my last interview with the Headmaster before I was expelled for the third time.

And then I noticed there was a strange little man sitting in a chair in the corner of the room with a pad and notebook. It was much as I imagined an interview with the Gestapo would be, but without the bright lamp shining in my eyes and presumably no cigarette burns to get the truth out of me...

'Your accountants have shown you my letter, have they?'

'Yes.'

'What have you to say?'

'I don't understand any of it.'

'Come, come, Mr Bannister.' He had a thick Welsh accent. I definitely felt xenophobic. First a Scotsman and now a Welshman! 'You're a businessman. We see from your file that you have bought several companies and sold many assets. But you have not put in any tax returns for the last year.'

'But... but I leave all that sort of thing to my accountants.'

'Maybe, but it is your responsibility to see that the returns are made.'

'But why is the tax so much? You say in your letter that it's over one million!'

'Well, you remember some years ago you bought the shares in a company called Reliable Grocers Limited and sold them three years later at what I can only call a gigantic profit?'

I remembered it well and still felt a rosy glow at the success.

'According to our records you failed to roll over the capital gain in time, so it attracts tax.'

'But I'm sure I did. It was all planned. I rolled the proceeds into Your Own Deli Limited. I didn't do quite so well out of that!'

'But you did not roll over within the statutory three year period.'

'I'm sure I did.'

'Not according to our information and that is why there is so much tax to pay. Apart from the tax due on the sale of Reliable Grocers Limited, I've assessed your last year's tax and included a provisional sum for the fines and interest due. You had better go into the matter with your accountants. I shall want another meeting with you when the partner dealing with your affairs returns from holiday.'

I waited until I got back to my office until I phoned Jim. I didn't want to be seen or heard yelling into my mobile in the street.

'Okay, okay, Greg. Calm down! I personally had nothing to do with all this. I'll have to look into it.'

The next few days were hell. I had nobody to talk to but Ann. She was trying to teach me how to use the computer but I found it difficult to concentrate. She was a nice woman but I didn't I feel I could discuss my financial problems with her. Oh, if only Cristabel or Dr Greenbaum were around!

'Ah, Cristabel, you're back at last. I've been phoning you... May I come and see you, please? I'm in more trouble and don't think I can cope!'

'It doesn't surprise me. Why didn't you let me help you? Anyhow, what's the trouble?'

'It's not just the bank and Toy Boy – now the Revenue say I owe them a million pounds.'

'Well okay, you can come over, but I must tell you I met

someone while I was in France, after you'd left, and we're engaged. So... well... it alters things a bit.'

'Bloody hell!' I thought. 'That's all I need on top of anything else, Cristabel getting married!'

I don't think I'd ever felt really jealous before. Whilst she'd been distant and reserved, I'd still felt she was somehow mine.

She looked radiant as she stood in the doorway of her studio. There was a huge diamond ring on the third finger of her left hand.

'I must congratulate you,' I said, kissing her on the cheek for the first time. 'Lovely ring, too. Is he rich?'

'Yes, he's an Italian. We met at Mass in Aix Cathedral. What do you want from me, Gregory?'

'I had hoped for a bit of sympathy and help.'

'How did this tax business happen?'

'I don't know. I always left everything to my accountants but I had a vague feeling that something was wrong.'

'I don't think I've ever had a letter from your accountants, but I haven't opened all your mail since I came back from France.'

'Now that you're back in action and I am getting married very shortly, I'd better stop acting as your attorney. I don't want to be unsympathetic but I think you must rely on professional help to sort out your trouble and of course talk to Dr Greenbaum. Over there are two box files full of letters to you together with copies of my replies The unopened letters are on top of them. Perhaps you would like to take them away with you!'

I knew I was being dismissed!

I shrugged my shoulders. 'Well thank you for dealing with everything for me,' I said.

As I left, I glanced around her studio for the last time. It smelt strongly of cigarette smoke as usual and was very tidy, but there was no canvas on the easel. I turned and sadly made my way down all those flights of stairs that I knew so well.

On my way home in the taxi I picked up the top file and started to glance through it. Almost immediately I came to a letter written back in January from an address in Knightsbridge. It read:

'Dear Gregory,

When I came to see you at Brook Street, as I promised, the place was locked up and in darkness. I've left messages on your answering service, but there is no reply. Please, please, let me know where you are and how you are.

Love from Jane (Jennings).'

The copy of the reply from Cristabel was dated some days later:

'Dear Ms Jennings,

Gregory Bannister is extremely unwell and is at present being cared for in a nursing home. He should not on any account be contacted or disturbed for the foreseeable future. I am acting as his attorney.

Cristabel Ashton.'

Then there was a pencil note at the bottom of the reply: 'Jane came to see me. Gave her the brush-off and told her not to phone again.'

'Dr Greenbaum, I'm in great trouble!'

'Vhy is zat?'

I told him all about the bank and being harassed by the new manager, and the claim by HMRC for £1 million.

'Do you zink zis claim is correct?'

'I don't know. I hope not. My accountants have obviously

made a mess of things and I'm sure they advised me there would be no tax to pay on the money from Reliable Grocers because I had rolled-over in time.'

'Vell, I do not understand zis "roll-over", but never mind. Do you not have assets vorth a million?'

'Maybe. But it's the aggro, you see. I don't think I can take it!'

'I understand zat, but do you not have assets worth a million?'

'I suppose the lease of my office and flat may be worth more than that. It's twenty-five years at a low rent. But I've got to live somewhere. The Toy Boy flat over the shop in Wood Green is vacant but I don't really fancy living in it. Dr Greenbaum, generally I'm in a terrible mess. Ever since I tried to turn over the new leaf, things have got even worse.'

'And vot is happening about zeez bank loans?'

I told him and rambled on about feeling empty and ill and not being able to cope, my holiday in France, my quarrel with Cristabel and that she was now getting married to an Italian.

'Maybe it was because of the row with you that she got engaged to ze Italian?'

I sent a sort of timetable to McGinger, the bank manager, saying that my solicitors had issued redundancy notices to the staff of Toy Boy. The auction of the stock would take place on a certain day and I was marketing the properties. The buyer I had had lined up for two of the properties had, of course, lost interest while I was ill. I sent a case of wine to Horace. I didn't want to work from Toy Boy's offices. I didn't think I'd be popular there at the moment! Wally was still on holiday. I kept turning over in my mind whether this claim by the Revenue could possibly be right, but I knew worrying about it was futile. I couldn't really make any progress until

Wally returned and his partner Jim steadfastly refused to do anything in the meantime.

Meanwhile, I was slowly reading through the two large files of letters. Cristabel had been very good and made the most meticulous notes of everything she had done. I didn't know what to feel about her. She'd helped me a great deal, but why? Did she pity me, or did she just like to control people? Or was it just her good nature or maybe her religion? Anyhow, she'd deserted me now. I felt terrible and had to keep lying down. Fortunately there wasn't much work to do, just clearing up bits and pieces from previous deals. I filled in the time by continuing to read through the files I had been given by Cristabel. Jane, in spite of the 'brush-off' from Cristabel, had written two further letters to me at Brook Street that had been redirected to Cristabel, hoping I was getting better and that 'my attorney would make sure I read this'. Then I came across a further letter from her from a different address, this time in Shropshire:

'Dear Gregory,
    I've come to live in the country with my father as he is not at all well. So when you have recovered, perhaps you could contact me here.
    Love, Jane.'

Jane obviously didn't give up easily! Her father apparently lived at a place called Netwyn Hall in Shropshire. I decided to phone her immediately.

'Gregory – it's you!'

'Yes, it's me.'

'You're better?'

'Well, a bit. I've only just been given your very nice letters, so I thought I'd phone you.'

'But where are you and how are you really?'

'At my office. I've had to get better because I've got serious financial difficulties to sort out.'

'I was very worried about what was happening to your business, but that friend of yours, Cristabel – is she a relation or something? – kept giving me the brush-off. I even went to her studio once. Very beautiful, but very frosty!'

'Spot on. No, she's not a relation. I haven't got any.'

'I see... Look, I can't come and see you because I've got to stay near Dad. But you could come here for a weekend if you liked!'

'How very kind. That would be very nice. But what about your father?'

'He's in hospital at the moment. Why don't you come this weekend. I'll be all on my own, apart from the staff.'

God, I felt grateful, but I marvelled at little Jane in a large country house with staff. How very odd! And how very kind of her to ask me. Not quite like taking me home to her flat after the dinner but the same sort of thing. She really must like me. Well, that was a distinct boost after the loss of Cristabel!

I took the train to Shrewsbury and Jane met me at the station. It was a lovely hot September Friday afternoon and she was wearing jodhpurs and a white cotton jumper. I noticed immediately she had a very neat little figure. She came up to me and peered closely into my face.

'Oh dear, you do look so thin and pale,' she said. 'Let me take your bag. I've got the Land Rover over there in the car park.'

The Land Rover had two bales of hay in the back and I immediately smelt horses.

'Is your father very ill?'

'Yes, I'm afraid so. It's his heart. But he's quite cheerful and hopes to come out of hospital some day next week. So I don't need to go and see him this weekend!'

I was very impressed as we drove into the grounds of

Netwyn Hall. It was the sort of place I had dreamed of owning. The house was Georgian and set on top of a small incline, so that it had good views of the lovely rolling hills of Shropshire on all sides. The drive wound up to the house slowly in a succession of gentle bends. The grounds were like old-fashioned parkland with mature oak and ash trees and a herd of deer. Beside the drive there were flower beds, all still full of summer bedding plants.

'Beautiful!' I said to Jane. 'How do you stop the deer eating the flowers?'

'Ah, that's a secret,' she replied, turning and smiling at me.

That weekend she treated me as an invalid, although I tried to convince her that I was much better.

'But how can you recover so suddenly?'

'Well, I've more or less had to.' And I told her everything about the bank loans and the tax demand. She was very quiet and sympathetic about it all.

'Good God! How awful for you,' was all she said.

I explained how Cristabel had taken it upon herself to put me into her aunt's nursing home and look after my affairs.

'She must like you – very much indeed!'

'Well, she's just got engaged to marry someone else.'

At this Jane merely said, 'I see,' and raised her small eyebrows above the top of her glasses. She was showing me all round the estate. It had the lot! It was the indulgence of a very wealthy man. Swimming pools both indoors and outside. A sauna, a billiard room, and of course stables with several horses.

'There's also the farm, but I don't suppose you're interested in that.'

Gradually it dawned on me who Jane's father must be.

'Is your father Lord Jennings of Jennings House Builders?' I asked.

'Well, yes.'

'How long ago did your mother die?'

'Two years ago. Dad's never been the same since. He didn't get married until he was nearly fifty. I think he must have been a bit of a playboy.' She said this looking sideways at me, I noticed. 'I think he wanted a son to carry on the family firm, but all he got was me and I've never been interested in business. As Dad quite rightly says, what good is a PhD in Medieval French Literature for running a house-building business?'

'Is that what you've got, then?'

'Yes, earlier this year.'

'Goodness,' I said, wiping my brow at the thought. But Jane interpreted this as my feeling tired.

'I think you'd better lie down before dinner,' she said. 'There's only the two of us and I've asked the cook for something simple. And perhaps you'd like to go riding tomorrow with me?'

As she drove me to the station late on Sunday afternoon, she asked, 'I suppose you wouldn't like to come again next weekend? I'm rather lonely here on my own. Dad may or may not be out of hospital by then.'

'Well, I've no other plans,' I said.

It seemed that Jane had taken over Cristabel's role of looking after me!

But, as I said to myself on the train back to London, she's simply not my type. She's only about 5 foot 2 inches tall, no curves, short mousy hair, often wears glasses. Her face is quite pretty when she smiles but she doesn't do that very often. She's serious and intellectual. But she obviously likes me. And apparently I did keep kissing her that night in the restaurant when I was drunk so I must have found her slightly attractive. Probably knowing myself at the time I'd have run my hands all over her body – but I had no recollection of what I thought of it!

7

First thing on Monday morning I had a phone call from Jim, the accountant.

'Not good news I'm afraid, Greg. Wally's been taken ill while on holiday and confessed to his wife that his work is in a terrible mess. She told us and we've been going through his files over the weekend. We're going to have to refer several things to our negligence insurance, including your tax affairs.'

'Well, I'm very sorry for Wally,' I replied, 'but I suppose that means the insurers will be paying the tax for me?'

'It's not quite as straightforward as that I'm afraid. It will take some time. You'll be getting a formal letter about it all in due course.'

I suppose I should have felt happier that the accountants had made a mistake and it was likely that the insurers would pay up; but I didn't. I suppose it was the uncertainty of everything.

I went to see Dr Greenbaum, feeling in need of some guidance.

'What should I do now?' I asked him.

'You must get zome good advice from zomeone. I am neither an accountant nor a lawyer.'

'Looks as if you'll have to sell your flat and office, Greg,' George said. 'I can't see the Revenue waiting while it's all sorted out. And I don't suppose the bank will lend you any more money.'

'But it's my home!'

'What about living in that flat over the Toy Boy shop in Wood Green? It's vacant and you could sell the shop subject to your tenancy.'

'I thought of that, but Wood Green is hardly Mayfair, is it?'

George mumbled something about 'desperate remedies'.

That was on Wednesday. After lying on my bed all afternoon and churning everything round in my mind and stomach, I phoned Jane.

'Jane, I really want to talk to you. It all seems to be getting worse. Could I possibly come up a bit earlier please?'

'When would you like to come? Dad's still in hospital.'

'As soon as you can have me! I feel you'll know what I should do.'

'Well, I hope you're not asking for business advice. As I said, I'm not good at that!'

'But you're very sensible.'

I arrived on Thursday afternoon, having cancelled my session on Friday morning with Dr Greenbaum. As the train drew in to Shrewsbury it was raining hard, a sudden fierce shower. I got out of the carriage with my bag, feeling utterly miserable, and stood on the platform under cover as Jane came towards me. She got soaked running from the car park and her blouse was sticking to her shoulders and her short mousy hair was dripping. She laughed as she met me, took off her spectacles and shook the water off them.

'Bit of a downpour. Better wait here a moment. It will soon pass over.' She shivered a little.

Then, as we got into the Land Rover, 'Do you mind if I take this wet blouse off and put my jumper on? You can look away if you want, but no doubt you've seen a girl in a bra before!'

It was done in a flash. Of course, I couldn't help having a quick glance. Pale, almost white skin, and two small but well-rounded breasts.

It was very comforting to be at Netwyn Hall again.

While the housekeeper was instructed to bring some tea and cakes, Jane disappeared to dry off properly.

'What am I to do, Jane?' I asked after she returned, when I'd told her about Wally and the insurance claim.

'Just go through all the financial stuff slowly again for me, please – right from the beginning. Tell me everything in detail.'

After I'd finished she said, 'It's amazing that you're managing as well as you are. You've had a really bad time. Tell me, why did your friend Cristabel, well... this is how it seems to me anyway... why did she take your life over? She's getting married now, you say. May I ask, were you lovers?'

'No. She never let me touch her, although I wanted to, sometimes desperately. You met her. She's very beautiful.'

'Yes... very. Is she a very well-known artist?'

'No, not particularly I don't think, although her pictures seem to me very colourful. That's why I bought two of them for my reception. But she did, I'm sure, want to help me. As I told you, she had me to stay almost every weekend.'

'Well, I can't comment. And Dr Greenbaum, was he someone she arranged for you?'

'Not quite. But she was very insistent I went to him.'

'And her aunt's nursing home... '

We went through the whole saga of Cristabel.

'Were you in love with her?'

'I think I was. Maybe still am. But it was hopeless. She was so kind but in a very distant and cold way. And it's bizarre that now she's getting married to someone she's only known for a few weeks!'

'Yes, well, I think that you must look at the whole thing as being in the past. Do you have a clear letter from the accountants saying that the proceeds from Reliable Grocers would be rolled over'

'Oh yes. In fact, I have it with me in my bag. I was reading it again on the train. I'll show it to you if you like.'

I brought the letter down to dinner and gave it to her to read.

'It seems pretty unequivocal that the insurers will have to pay up in due course. As you can see, Dad and I are not exactly poor. It seems so drastic selling your office and your home to keep the Revenue quiet. Would you let me make you a temporary loan?'

I was flabbergasted. I remember gulping and almost choking on a piece of potato I had in my mouth at the time.

'Don't decide now,' she said, 'sleep on it and tell me in the morning. I'd like to help. You've had such bad luck.'

I remember tossing and turning all night long and having had hardly any sleep. In the past I had had all these glamorous girlfriends upon whom I lavished expensive meals, holidays and gifts and since I'd been ill, the position had been completely reversed. First I had been looked after by Cristabel and now Jane, who was offering to make me a huge loan. God, it felt awful somehow.

'Well, what do you think?' Jane asked at breakfast.

'You mean about the loan?'

'Of course,' she said, smiling at me.

'It's terribly kind of you but I don't think I can possibly accept it, Jane. Since my father died I've always worked on my own and tried to be self-reliant. Even though things are very bad at the moment I feel I must try to stand on my own two feet.'

I could tell immediately that my decision had upset her. Her smile faded.

'Can I not persuade you? It will probably mean you'll have to sell your office and flat.'

'Yes, it probably will, but if that's what it takes… ' I said.

'I see. Well, in an hour or two I shall have to leave you to your own devices until teatime. I have to go and see Dad in hospital.'

That was on Saturday. It turned out she had to go and visit her father for several hours on Sunday as well!

As she drove me to the station late on Sunday afternoon, she said, 'Well, if you're determined to sell the office, why don't you ask your friend Jasper if he knows anyone who wants it? It's sort of in his line, I think, and I presume you will want a quick sale.'

'Really bad luck, my boy! Look, if you are really serious about selling your place I'll put you in touch with my young nephew, Joshua. It's just the sort of pad he's looking for.'

And so, after a lot of haggling (Joshua was very like his uncle), I did a quick sale to Joshua for £1.4 million to include most of the furniture. I know I could have got more on the open market.

I went to George for financial advice, as I could no longer use my accountants. He told me he thought that as I would have the money in hand I should pay the Revenue the whole of what they demanded for the time being and send the rest to the bank, keeping back enough to pay off my personal overdraft (which I still hadn't sorted out) and keep a further bit back for my expenses.

'If you don't pay the Revenue soon I bet they'll sting you with penalties and interest. They're like that!' he concluded.

Whether George's advice was good or not I wasn't sure, but by that stage I was almost beyond caring. I did what he suggested.

It was a very, very sad day when I moved from Brook Street, my home and workplace for ten years, into the flat over the shop in Wood Green. It was rather grim and needed redecorating. It had one largish sitting room, a bedroom, kitchen and bathroom. The previous tenant had left behind most of his furniture, and I'm not surprised. It was old and battered. But as I hoped I wouldn't be there too long, I decided to make do.

The redundancies for the Toy Boy staff were dealt with very quickly. The auction of the stock took place as arranged. The proceeds were very disappointing – less than book value. Then I had a rare piece of luck. I managed to sell Toy Boy's office, which I'd never used. This did mean that I had to set up my office in the flat, but it removed another liability and this pleased the bank manager. He'd also been pleased with the balance of the money from the sale of Brook Street, but nevertheless he still wrote me a letter insisting that the shops and the warehouse were sold by the end of the year – otherwise he would have to take further steps. This really worried me.

I dispensed with Ann and settled down to a life of austerity. I instructed five different estate agents to try and sell the three shops and the warehouse and worked from the flat with my mobile phone, a laptop computer (which Ann had more or less taught me to use before she left) and one or two other items of office equipment I'd taken from Toy Boy's offices before sending the rest of the contents to the sale room. I told Dr Greenbaum that I couldn't afford to go on seeing him.

He wished me 'good luck'.

In all, it didn't seem quite the end of the world, but almost.

But now, re-enter Cristabel.

It was a horrible wet Saturday, early November, late afternoon, and I was watching some rugby match on the tv that I didn't really care about when Cristabel called me.

'Gregory, please may I come and see you?'

'Well, yes of course, if you really want to. Do we have something to talk about still?'

'Yes, I want to see you and talk to you.'

'Well, okay. By the way I've moved. I had to sell the place in Brook Street. I'm in Wood Green... '

'I'd like to come now.'

'Of course.' I gave her the address.

When I went down the narrow staircase to the street door after she rang the bell, I had a premonition that something awful had happened to Cristabel. It somehow penetrated the door and pushed its way up the staircase to meet me. And when I opened the door and saw her, I knew I was right. Her face was grey, her hair obviously unwashed and she staggered as she walked up the stairs in front of me.

To try and jolly her up I said, 'As you can see, I've come down in the world. Sit over there. It's the least uncomfortable of the chairs. I hope you don't mind me saying, but you don't look very well – shall I make you some tea?'

'Later, and then I'll ask you how you come to be here. But first I want to tell you what's happened to me.'

'Are you not married yet?'

'No, and never shall be now. I've come to you because I thought you were the one person I knew who might understand what I have done.'

I sat down opposite her. She hadn't taken her coat off and she sat with her hands between her knees and her head hanging down. Then she suddenly flicked her head up and looked straight at me.

'I've just had an abortion,' she said.

'Ah, I see!' was all I could think of saying.

'You remember I told you I was engaged to an Italian I met in the Cathedral at Aix?'

'I could hardly forget it!'

'Well, I was a naïve fool. He gave me an expensive engagement ring and on the basis that we would be married in Italy within three weeks, persuaded me to go and stay with him at a villa he has in Monte Carlo. But all he wanted to do was to get me into bed. After he'd done everything he wanted to me for a fortnight he suddenly announced that we couldn't get married after all. His father had come home to Italy from South America and said if he married an English girl and not someone from his very large, extended family, he would be disinherited. Of course, I didn't believe him and we had a terrible row. Then, when I came back to England, I discovered I was pregnant. So I had an abortion.'

She sat looking at me with tears trickling down her cheeks.

'Why didn't you keep the baby?'

'Because I didn't want to give birth to that bastard's child!' she shouted. 'It would have probably been just like him – a liar and a cheat!'

'Why didn't you use contraception…? Oh, that's a silly question.'

'And abortion is killing!' she shouted at me again.

'Not everybody thinks so.'

'Oh God, I feel awful. I feel so bad I can't even smoke!'

'Did he know you were pregnant?'

'No.'

'Have you told your mother or Auntie?'

'Of course not. I came to you. I had to tell someone. I knew you wouldn't be shocked.'

I did feel shocked but didn't say so. The whole thing seemed so unlike the Cristabel I knew.

'Let me make you some tea now.'

When I came back, she still hadn't taken her coat off, but was curled up and seemed almost asleep on a terrible imitation leather sofa that the previous tenant had left behind. But she opened her eyes and held out her hand for the cup.

'Do you mind if I stay for a little while?' she said.

After a time I realised that the 'little while' would mean 'quite a while'. She was in some state of awful shock for want of a better description. She lay on the sofa, hardly moving.

I eventually persuaded her to stand up and put my arms round her to try to console her. But she didn't respond. She seemed completely immersed in her own misery. Not knowing really what to do for the best I managed to get her to my bed, tried to make her comfortable and then pulled up a chair. She slept most of the time. At about ten o'clock I lay down myself on the awful sofa, with a cushion under my head and my coat over my body as I hadn't got a spare blanket. I think it was one of the worst nights I ever spent. I was very worried about Cristabel. I suggested I should call a doctor but she just grasped my hand and said, 'No, no, Gregory, please no. I'll be all right. This is just emotional. The clinic said I was physically okay but might feel depressed and upset. I came to you because I couldn't stand being on my own.'

I went into the bedroom every hour. Twice, Cristabel wanted to go to the bathroom. She was so shaky that I had to help her undress and support her. I felt so sorry for her that I didn't feel the squeamish revulsion I normally have for bodily functions.

At about eight o'clock the next morning I tried to get her to eat some Cornflakes and drink some of the coffee I had made for myself.

She managed a few spoonfuls of cereal and then announced that she was going to be sick.

I helped her to the bathroom just in time. I thought to myself, as I practically carried her back to bed, that I had so often longed to have physical contact with her body, but this physical contact was something entirely different. She had the most beautiful body but I felt nothing sexual, only great pity that she was so upset and ill.

Once I had got her settled down I said, 'Look, you're obviously feeling very bad and I don't know that I can look after you properly. You ought to be in a nursing home or something. Can't I arrange it with Auntie?'

She grasped my hand again and said, 'No, please, please, Gregory! Just let me stay here a little while longer. You don't mind, do you?'

'Of course not,' I said. 'You looked after me. But if you're going to stay here I must go out and buy you some things once the shops open. I'll have to leave you for a short while. Will you be all right?'

'Yes, just leave a bucket beside me in case of accidents.'

It was Sunday and so the shops didn't open until about eleven. I wondered, as I walked through the drizzly rain, why on earth Cristabel had come to me. Had she really no female friend she could rely on? Maybe she was so distant with everyone that she didn't have many friends at all. I had never noticed during the weekends I had spent with her that anyone phoned her. Having to look after her was about the last thing I wanted at that time. I felt utterly low and depressed, but I suppose she took my mind off my own troubles.

I bought her two pairs of pyjamas, a dressing gown and a packet of knickers. And I bought a small folding bed for myself with a sleeping bag and pillow, all of which I collected later in the afternoon and manhandled back to the flat with some difficulty.

I had to help her change and then sat by her bed holding her hand, which she seemed to like. She hardly ever spoke.

And so I looked after her as well as I could. This involved helping her shower, washing her hair, and all the other intimate things that nurses do so well but I'm sure I did very badly. And she gradually got better and started to look like Cristabel again. Five days after she'd first arrived, she said she thought she ought to go home and could I please order her a taxi to take her to her studio in Fulham? In some ways I was relieved; I was feeling very tired. Quite exhausted.

Before she left, she solemnly shook me by the hand and said, 'Gregory, I am so grateful. You've looked after me wonderfully and for so long. I only intended to stay for an hour or two when I first came.'

'But you looked after me,' I said.

'I never had to change your pants for you or wash you. I'm sure God will reward you for your kindness to a sinner. Will you please promise never to tell *anyone* what I had to do?'

I promised.

The flat seemed very empty after she'd gone. Although she said she'd phone me, she didn't. I rang her many times but always just got her answering service. I think those five days were the most bizarre in my life.

8

I had been trying to sell the three shops and the warehouse since the beginning of September and the end of November was now fast approaching. McGinger was conducting a sort of terrorist campaign against me. Every week he sent me a bank statement setting out my total indebtedness. So, reluctantly, I had gradually disposed of all the racehorses and the Aston Martin – all at dismal prices. I had finally made myself go through my personal bank account statements and my credit cards bills for the previous two years. But everything was in such a muddle that I eventually gave up. My spending had been profligate and careless. I had relied on Gloria to keep a check on things but she obviously hadn't bothered much. Maybe she'd been helping herself. But I wouldn't be able to prove it, so I decided to forget it all and concentrate on the future; I made a firm resolution that I would never let my finances get in such a mess again. I would make a note of everything I spent and check my bank and credit card statements every month. I also resolved that if ever I had a girlfriend again, I would 'ration' my spending on her.

I think it was during this period that it really hit me how dependent I'd been in the past on having a young woman 'in tow', as my father used to say. And I suppose Gloria was a kind of 'woman in tow' as well, in her own way.

Because I was still taking both antidepressants and anti-anxiety pills, each of which said 'avoid alcohol' on the box, I tried to limit my intake to two glasses of wine a day. I had given up the cigars completely.

For the first time in my life since leaving school, I had spare time. Too much of it! I watched rubbish on the television, read a few detective novels, played with my computer and wandered about Wood Green and other parts of North London I'd never been to before, like Muswell Hill and Alexandra Park. I seemed to have no desire to go to the theatre or the cinema. My main meal was generally a kebab from one of the numerous takeaways in the area. They were cheap and tasty.

I had lots of time to think about my past life. In particular, I thought a great deal about Cristabel. A strange person; so distant with me, and probably everyone else, and then suddenly being seduced by an Italian she'd just met in a cathedral who offered her marriage. What had suddenly come over her? And then coming to me to be looked after! And now she was avoiding me. I suppose I still hoped that she would suddenly phone up and be nice to me – whatever being 'nice' might mean.

And I thought of Jane's generosity. I'd probably been very churlish in refusing her offer of a loan and I hadn't heard from her since that day. I had obviously seriously upset her. I hadn't liked to phone her, but I was disappointed that she hadn't been in touch with me. I'd hoped she might have wanted to find out what had happened about the sale of Brook Street and how I was getting on.

One Saturday there was a day of freak weather. After two weeks of November gloom, the sun shone and it was warm, almost hot. Along with several thousand other people I decided to go to Alexandra Park. In particular, I liked the views over London on a clear day. I managed to find a spare space on a park bench and looked around. The place was heaving: it was multi-racial and multi-cultural, scores of children playing with balls and the smaller ones in buggies or toddling. I realised that my previous high lifestyle had insulated me from all this – the real world for lots of Londoners. People who had very little money, who couldn't afford taxis and struggled to afford their weekly shopping. Life on benefits. My own financial security was in doubt and might be forever, if I couldn't sell the shops and warehouse.

But there was only one day of sunshine before the gloom returned.

Then, out of the monotony, two things happened on the same day. The first was a phone call from a solicitor called Mrs Bostock. She explained she was acting for my accountants' insurers and wondered if she could please come and look at my files. I said I had no objection but I had to go and get the files out of storage, where I had put all the stuff from Brook Street that wouldn't fit into the flat.

The second was a call from one of the five firms of estate agents I had instructed to sell the three shops and the warehouse. I could hardly believe it when they said they thought they had found a purchaser – a company selling computers and mobile phones – for the whole lot. The price being offered was of course considerably less than my asking price. But it would solve my problems with the bank and I was feeling quite cheerful when a few days later, Mrs Bostock arrived very promptly at the time appointed to look at the files. She wasn't what I expected – I don't really know what I expected but certainly it wasn't someone like Mrs Bostock. Underneath her thick, green overcoat she was an extremely elegant and well-endowed little blonde (natural I think) lady in a neat, grey business suit and high heels. The chap who accompanied her was apparently an accountant; and looked just like one.

I put the files on the dining table in the sitting room and

asked them if they minded if I worked at the computer while they looked through them. Not that I had any work to do, but I found looking at things on Google kept me occupied.

'By the way,' I said, 'as I told you I've no objection, but why do you want to look at these files?'

'Because your accountants' files are in a terrible mess. We have a suspicion that the Revenue have somehow made a mistake and you did roll over in time!'

'Well, I sincerely hope you're right... Would you like a cup of coffee?'

'I think I can see what's happened here,' Mrs Bostock said after she and the accountant had spent half an hour shuffling through my files with furious concentration and muttering to one another. 'Undoubtedly you rolled over the proceeds within the three year period, according to everything we can see here, but your accountants put the wrong date on your tax return, which is also in the file. Presumably you never checked the copy they sent you?'

'I don't suppose I did!'

'I'll go back to the office now and try and set up a meeting with the Revenue,' she said.

'Will they accept that the accountants made a mistake?'

'I shall do my damndest to make sure they do!' she said fiercely. 'I shall be in touch again soon, Mr Bannister.'

And she was. She telephoned two days later and said she'd got a date for the meeting in a week's time and would like me to be available to attend. She explained that she needed to come and make copies of various letters and documents on my files and had I a photocopier? Well, yes I had. It was one of the things I brought from Toy Boy's office – a small portable one I kept in a cupboard that proved very useful from time to time.

So, Mrs Bostock visited again, on her own this time.

Unfortunately (or fortunately) the electric cable to the photocopier wouldn't reach my desk or the table so it had to be used on the floor. I apologised about this to Mrs Bostock for whom I felt a great deal of warmth – apart from her physical attributes - as she was going to try to get the Revenue to change its mind and I was very grateful.

'Look,' I said as she arrived, 'I can't go on calling you Mrs Bostock. What's your first name? Mine's Gregory.'

'Mrs Bostock is just fine.'

'But you must have a first name. What does your husband call you?'

'He doesn't call me anything any longer. He died a year ago of a heart attack while playing squash. And don't commiserate too much. We weren't getting on at all well and if he'd lived, I suspect we'd be divorced by now! But if you must, you can call me Elizabeth.'

'What a tough nut!' I thought, but said, 'I'm sorry... I've put the files on the table again but I'm afraid you have to kneel on the floor to use the photocopier as the flex won't reach the table. I'll do the copying if you like.'

'No problem… I'll do it myself. Your solicitors fortunately sent you copies of all the contracts so I can copy them and various other relevant letters and the tax return.'

And with that she kicked off her high heels, hitched up her skirt and knelt down by the photocopier.

Elizabeth kneeling by the photocopier with her skirt hitched up was almost irresistible. For the first time since I'd been ill, I felt a surge of my old lustful feelings. What I had felt for Cristabel had been different. This was an urgent and base need. I had always been fortunate to have a willing girlfriend but I could understand why men needed to seek relief from prostitutes when overcome with this sort of desire.

'I want to be a bit theatrical about this,' she said once she'd finished the photocopying. 'I'll go into the meeting with the photocopies, but I want you to be waiting outside with these three files I've put on the floor just in case they want to read all through them and question you. And would you please be smartly dressed for the meeting. I have to say you look a little scruffy today. I'll see myself out.'

After she'd gone I looked at myself in the bathroom mirror. Yes, I saw what she meant. I had 'let myself go' a bit. I hadn't had a haircut for some time and I'd taken to wearing an open-necked shirt and a cardigan with a pair of old flannel trousers as I worked from the flat.

I would hardly appeal to her looking like that.

Although I had boldly asserted to Jane that I must stand on my own two feet, I was very anxious most of the time. So I fortified myself with anti-anxiety pills before the meeting with the tax man. But I still felt nervous and was sweating slightly as I sat beside Elizabeth in the same awful waiting room. I was suitably dressed with my hair cut and my files in my best leather briefcase. Elizabeth looked stunning; a trifle more make-up than usual and emanating a heavy perfume. I wondered if that might set the dour Welsh inspector against her.

We didn't have to wait too long before Elizabeth was asked to come in. So I sat and hoped, whilst Elizabeth's perfume lingered in the air. I tried to doze off but the chair was so uncomfortable that it was impossible. I had intended to bring a newspaper to read, but had forgotten. The waiting room didn't have any magazines. The meeting seemed to be going on for ever. Then there was the turning of the tax man's door handle – he was actually showing Elizabeth out of his office.

'So nice to meet you, Mrs Bostock. Many thanks for your help in resolving all this.'

Elizabeth arrived by my side with a broad smile.

'It's okay?'

'Yes, they've accepted it. You will be repaid that part of your tax bill ASAP. It will be about £700,000.'

'I'm very, very grateful for what you've done for me,' I said touching her arm.

'Gregory, I'm pleased at the outcome but you must remember that I was doing it to save my clients money and not for you.'

'Nevertheless, I'm greatly in your debt and as now it's nearly half-past twelve, will you let me take you out to lunch?'

She looked at her watch. 'Okay. But it will have to be a quick one. I'm very busy.'

During the lunch she told me she was only twenty-eight and hoping to be made a partner in her firm very soon. That was why she was so keen to get a good result, and obviously was very pleased with the success of the interview with the tax man.

'That was not the sort of splendid meal I should buy you for what you've done,' I said. 'Can we organise something better in due course?'

'Yes, that would be lovely. Give me a ring on my mobile – here's the number on my business card. I must go now.'

When I got back to my flat, there was an email from the estate agents to say they had now agreed terms with the prospective purchasers but they wanted a quick exchange of contracts and completion to catch the pre-Christmas trade. They would also want vacant possession of my flat!

The relief of getting the tax back and selling the properties was immense but a quick calculation showed me that because of the low price I would receive for the properties and the long period of paying interest to my bank, I would only make a very small profit out of Toy Boy.

One is never satisfied!

I walked round the streets of Wood Green trying to come to terms with it all – the end of the Toy Boy affair and me moving on to a new phase in my life. I resolved that I must try to put all my troubles behind me insofar as I could. The bank would be happy now and I would be solvent again but there was something stopping me from feeling as relieved, or even jubilant, as I should have done.

While I was in the turmoil of trying to move, Cristabel phoned. She said she was sorry not to have answered any of my messages but she had been frantically busy reorganising her life. She suggested we should meet for lunch at a small French restaurant we both knew in the West End, so that she could explain everything.

She was sitting at the table when I arrived. If I had not seen her so ill after the abortion, I would never have known what she'd been through. She looked as lovely as ever and I wanted to kiss her, but as I bent down towards her face she put the back of her hand up so that I had to kiss that instead.

'Gregory, please. You know our relationship isn't like that. I shall always be so grateful to you for the way you looked after me and I've bought you a little present. I suppose it's a keepsake.' She put down a small parcel on the place mat where I would be sitting.

'Don't open it now. Take it home and open it there.'

I asked her how she felt.

'I think I'm fully recovered,' she said, 'as much as I ever shall be. The reason I haven't been in touch before is because Mummy is divorcing Daddy. He stayed with the twenty-year-old and Mummy and I are going to live together. We've found a nice house in Barnes by the river with a big attic room which I can use as a studio. Daddy is being very generous about money. I suppose he feels guilty, and so he should!'

I told her about my own good fortune; the tax refund and selling the properties.

'There you are, you see!' she said. 'I told you God would reward you.'

At the end of the lunch Cristabel said, 'Look Gregory, we've helped one another in the past but I think this meal should be the end of things between us. I want to make a fresh start and I think you should, too.'

When I got home, I opened the parcel and found it contained a small paperweight made of Perspex; inside the paperweight in small gold letters were the words 'Look Forward Not Back' with some sort of misty horizon behind the lettering.

It made me feel very sad, but I didn't like it very much and put it in a drawer. It must have been taken out with the junk furniture when I moved because I never saw it again.

George managed to get the contracts for the sale of all of the properties exchanged and completed in five days. My bank account was at last in credit as the Revenue repaid the tax with amazing speed. The only outstanding thing was how much more tax I actually owed the Revenue and if they would be repaying anything more.

I had a strong desire to have a meeting with McGinger at the bank and tell him what a prick I thought he was – but I decided against it. It might relieve my feelings but it wouldn't get me anywhere. Maybe he'd even done me a good turn by being so fierce with me and making me reduce my debt, although he made me feel horribly paranoid at the time. I quietly made arrangements to move my accounts to another bank, which gave me a great sense of satisfaction.

But I was homeless! Giving vacant possession of the flat meant that I had to move all the furniture. I hired a skip and threw most of it in there. I had brought one or two pieces with me from Brook Street, which I put into storage. I booked into a hotel and spent several days searching for a temporary home. All the suitable places wanted a year's tenancy, but I eventually found a nice one-bedroomed flat just off Sloane Square which was fully furnished and equipped. The owner only wanted to let it for three months while he 'wintered abroad', as his agents put it.

9

My time living in that flat near Sloane Square I remember as a sort of twilight period. The days were dark and the flat, although perfectly comfortable, was in a red brick Victorian building with small windows – probably rather gloomy even in midsummer. In December I had to keep the lights on all day. The building had originally been one rather grand house in the Edwardian era, no doubt with a butler and maids. Now it was divided (quite nicely) into five flats. Living there I felt completely anonymous – more so even than in the flat in Wood Green. I think you could have died one night and it might have been some months before your body was found.

I somehow knew my life would never be the same again. Although I was now solvent, there would be no return to the sort of days I'd spent with Zoë in New York and Los Angeles a year previously. I didn't feel exactly ill any more, but I certainly didn't feel very well. I really didn't know what to do with myself or how to pass the time. I had cleared up all the loose ends of my previous deals and I had no desire to try to embark on anything else. Maybe because I had nothing much to keep me occupied, I felt very anxious most of the time. I tried going to the races but just felt cold and miserable. I visited my club occasionally but came to the conclusion I didn't like it any more. A few members approached me to make mild enquiries about my health as they hadn't seen me for some time, but I didn't feel any of them were really that interested.

And I had great difficulty in stopping myself drinking.

I had of course, as expected, never heard anything from Cristabel. And more surprisingly, nothing from Jane, although she had my mobile number. I still couldn't bring myself to phone her. I don't quite know why. And so much time was passing that I wondered if I should ever speak to her again.

But I did call Elizabeth frequently to see how she was getting on dealing with the rest of my tax problems. But she obviously thought I was a nuisance and was steadfast about my taking her out to dinner. She said she was far too busy and working till late at night and at the weekends.

I suppose trying to meet Elizabeth became almost an obsession. I found myself thinking of her most of the time. But then I had nothing much else to think about, apart from what I was going to do in the future – and I had no answer to that.

I roamed around the streets hoping inspiration might come to me. The Christmas decorations were wonderful once darkness fell at around four o'clock. I often wandered up and down the Kings Road and Sloane Street hoping that I might meet somebody I knew, but I never did. I sat for hours in the numerous cafés in the area, drinking coffee that I didn't really want and reading newspapers.

I resolved that I must learn to cook for myself, as most of the eating places in the area seemed very expensive after the kebab houses of Wood Green. I bought a copy of a cookery book aimed at novices such as myself, but I couldn't summon up any enthusiasm for it and ended up buying expensive meals in the local restaurants.

Eventually, on the 18th December, Elizabeth phoned and said that if I was free I could take her out to dinner on Christmas Eve. She was going to spend Christmas Day with her divorcée sister and the sister's two children in Surbiton. Unfortunately for her, the sister and children were vegetarians so she would appreciate what she called a 'proper meal' on Christmas Eve.

I became ridiculously excited about the dinner. I was spending Christmas on my own, apart from an invitation from George (who was obviously taking pity on me) to have lunch on Boxing Day with him and his family in Finchley. Having once met George's wife, this was not an exhilarating prospect.

I had arranged with Elizabeth that I should take her to the Ritz in Piccadilly and that I would meet her outside the front entrance at eight. In view of her remarks about my appearance, I dressed in my best suit with a Hermes tie, and my smartest overcoat. I took two anti-anxiety pills. I had no idea what might happen after a lavish dinner on Christmas Eve!

Foolishly, I arrived about ten minutes early and hadn't realised how cold it would be waiting outside. Although the entrance is under a portico, an east wind was blowing down Piccadilly with a few flakes of snow in it. By eight-fifteen I was frozen. I didn't want to go inside into the lobby in case I should miss Elizabeth. I tried calling her but I just got a recorded message. I waited for another ten minutes and then phoned the restaurant to see if by any chance she'd walked past me or gone in by the other entrance. But no, she wasn't there. I was very upset. I explained my guest hadn't arrived and asked would they please cancel the booking. I suppose I should have waited a few more minutes, but I didn't. I remember shutting my mobile and putting it in my overcoat pocket, saying 'Sod her!' loudly and walking up Piccadilly in search of a pub. Before long I found what I was looking for; I had a double whisky and gradually started to thaw out. The bar was full of a strange assortment of people, some wearing paper party hats. A red-nosed man had one of those party blowers that makes a noise and uncurls, shoving it right into people's faces. When he came towards me, I turned my back.

'Okay, toff,' he shouted. 'Too posh for a lark are we?' I suppose I was better dressed than most of the people around me.

I left that pub, found another one nearby which was quieter, and had another large whisky. I didn't finish it as I started to feel nauseous; I should have known not to drink on top of the anti-anxiety pills. I went out into the cold again, the nausea intensifying, and walked towards Piccadilly Circus. There was a church nearby with a choir and brass band around a large Christmas tree, singing carols in the churchyard. It looked like a picture on a Christmas card – I even looked up to see if there might be any angels hovering in the sky. The words of the carol were almost blown away by the cold wind, but I knew them anyhow:

'God rest ye merry gentlemen.
Let nothing you dismay
Remember Christ our Saviour
Was born on Christmas Day
To save us all from Satan's power
When we were gone astray:
O, tidings of comfort and joy
Comfort and joy
O, tidings of comfort and joy!'

For some reason it reminded me of my mother and I felt like crying. Why had she so rarely bothered to come and see me? She obviously never loved me – and nor did anyone else.

I didn't know what to do. Although the feeling of sickness was wearing off, I didn't feel hungry. The sensible thing would have been to have hailed a taxi or hopped on a bus to Sloane Square. But perversely, I decided I would walk back to my flat. It wasn't that far. I'd got in some groceries for the holiday period and I could have a snack when I got home.

Nearing Hyde Park Corner, I remembered Jane had said I had staggered when she helped me home from the restaurant. How very odd it seemed that she'd taken me back to her flat; most women wouldn't have considered it proper. I hadn't really thought about that aspect of it before. I supposed I'd been so self-centred at the time, I'd assumed every woman would want to do anything for me. And now I was deserted by the only three I currently knew. Elizabeth had stood me up. Cristabel had dumped me and I had so upset Jane by refusing her kind offer of a loan that she hadn't spoken to me since. I told her that I must stand on my own feet. Well, I had managed to pay off my debts, but I felt utterly alone and deserted.

It was at that moment that I tripped and fell. I don't know if it was the whiskies, the pills, a feeling of hopelessness or the very slight fall of snow. I put my right hand out to save myself as I went down and felt a sharp pain in my wrist and then the rest of my body came into contact with what seemed the hardest pavement in all London. Strangely, there was nobody nearby. When I managed to lever myself up with my left hand, I noticed that I'd torn my trousers and my right wrist was hurting like hell.

'Yes, you've broken your wrist,' I was told some time later when my arm was being put into a sling. 'Could have been worse. Want to see the X-ray?'

I was in the Accident and Emergency of the same hospital I'd been in after fainting in church. And thanks to the marvels of modern technology, the X-ray was flashed up onto a screen over my bed. What I'd done to my wrist looked horrible. A bit of bone had become half detached from whatever the bone at the top of the wrist is called.

'It'll heal,' the doctor reassured me. 'Have you got someone at home to look after you? Will you be all right?'

'Of course,' I lied.

'We'll give you three packets of painkillers as it's the holiday period.'

They slung my jacket over my shoulders and my overcoat on top of that, and I left following the exit signs for the Fulham Road. I felt very cold. I suppose it was the shock.

This time, there was a black taxi waiting and thankfully I was soon back in my flat.

It was two o'clock and I hadn't had anything to eat. So, after I had shrugged off my overcoat and jacket, I tried to open a tin of soup. This proved impossible with my left hand only. I'm very 'right-handed'. Eventually, I found an open packet of ham and managed to make a sandwich, with some sliced bread. As making tea seemed far too complicated, I opened some whisky by holding the bottle between my legs and unscrewing the top with my left hand. No sooner had I got the top off than I thought about how terrible the whisky had made me feel earlier, but I didn't care. I half filled a tumbler with neat whisky and slurped it down. Strangely this time it made me feel much better, even happy! But the happiness didn't last. I had great difficulty in getting my trousers off. I couldn't even undo the front buttons of my shirt with my left hand. I collapsed on my bed and lay there worrying how I was going to be able to manage. I'd have to get a nurse to help me. But how? The flat wasn't wired up for Wi-Fi so I couldn't look up nursing agencies on my computer. There weren't any telephone directories. I supposed I could phone Directory Enquiries – but it was now Christmas Day. Nobody would be working.

Maybe it was the combination of the anti-anxiety pills, the painkillers and the whisky but I started to believe that my present situation must be some retribution for my past. I never believed in a God who looked down from the sky, pointing a finger at wrongdoers and punishing them. But here I was feeling terrible, helpless and depressed with a broken wrist and unable to cope. I'd led a selfish existence, just wanting to make more and more money and spend it on expensive cars and racehorses. I'd drunk too much and eaten too much. I'd screwed a succession of women and I'd let them screw me for everything they could get out of me: holidays, meals at smart restaurants, trips to the casino, expensive jewels – I'd even bought a specially favoured one a sports car. I would have probably avoided my recent financial difficulties if I hadn't spent so much money on them. But I had got tired of them all one by one, then suddenly Zoë had ditched me; that was the beginning of my troubles. The recent experiences with Cristabel, Jane and Elizabeth seemed even more bitter as I lay in bed with an aching wrist at two-thirty on Christmas morning in an anonymous flat. I didn't think there was anyone in any of the other flats in the building. They'd probably all gone away for Christmas – not that I'd ever seen anyone going in or out.

What was I going to do? My wrist was really hurting like hell again. I must get up and take two more painkillers. Well, I thought, as I swallowed the second of the painkillers, I can't phone Jane now, not for a few hours yet.

Then I realised that I had unconsciously made a decision; I choked and spat out the tablet.

Oh God, was that the only way out! I went and lay down again shivering and pulled the bedclothes round my neck. Eventually, I saw Christmas Day dawn through the chink in the curtains. I thought of the time when I'd been very small and believed in Father Christmas. There'd be my stocking filled by my mother at the end of my bed. It had been so nice when my mother had still been at home. It might have been okay for her to leave Dad, but did she have to leave me as well? Oh God! What I longed for was someone kind to look after me.

Eventually, at 9 o'clock I couldn't wait any longer and I phoned Jane. I had a speech beautifully rehearsed, but all

I got was her answering service. I couldn't possibly say my prepared speech to a recording so I rang off.

She'd probably gone away for Christmas.

But no – I presumed that was unlikely with her father still ill. Maybe she'd gone to visit him in hospital. But why didn't one of the staff answer the phone? There'd been four of them when I visited. Perhaps they were all given leave over Christmas?

But after a time, I couldn't just bear to lie there and do nothing and I had no mobile number for her. I tried again.

Still the answering service! What was I going to do if she never answered? I decided to try her number every fifteen minutes. That seemed the only thing to do. By ten-thirty I was almost desperate but at ten forty-five – 'Hello,' she said.

'Jane, it's Gregory.'

'Oh, Happy Christmas!'

I think I was so overcome I could hardly speak, but eventually I managed to say, 'Well, I'm afraid it's not very happy for me. I've been trying to get you since nine o'clock.'

'I've been out riding. It's a tradition with me for Christmas morning. But what's the matter?'

I told her how I'd broken my right wrist and was all alone in a flat in Chelsea and simply couldn't manage. There was quite a pause after I'd finished. Eventually she said, 'I see. Well, I'm very sorry and I'm very glad to hear from you. Can I be of practical if not financial help?'

A few hours later, I was sitting in front of a blazing log fire in what Jane calls the drawing room of Netwyn Hall.

And I have been sitting in front of the fire most of the time over the Christmas period, thinking about all that's happened to me over the past year. I have, of course, told Jane about selling my office and flat and how I've finally sorted out my financial affairs. She seems to have forgiven me.

Her father is at home and he has a resident nurse who has been also looking after me, although I'm sure from the way she's behaving, Jane would prefer to look after me herself.

I've had a few gentle walks round the grounds, always accompanied by Jane who seems to have an irrational fear that I might fall over again.

I have now also visited Lord Jennings in his bedroom.

'Please call me Bob, old chap,' were his first words to me.

He must be nearing eighty, or at least he looks it. By one of those strange coincidences he knew my father very well, apparently, when they were both young – he even did a couple of developments with him.

'I hear from Jane that you've had a run of very, very bad luck and had to sell your office and flat all because of a mistake by your accountants, but you're over it now. What are you planning to do in the future?'

I said I really didn't know. I'd been ill but was beginning to feel better.

'Yes, Jane's told me all about it. Quite a story. Look, how would you like to come and help run Jennings Homes? I've always controlled the thing myself but I know I'm not going to be able to do the day-to-day running of it in the future. Jane's simply not interested, although I think she has quite a good business brain.'

It was a very tempting offer. Rather like Jane's offer of the loan.

'Well, think about it Gregory and let me know how you feel about it say on New Year's Day. That's a good day for making decisions!'

I went and sat by the fire again and thought about it. I realised that the real reason I had turned down Jane's offer of a loan was the feeling that it would somehow tie me to her and this offer from her father had the same sort of string attached, although nothing was explicit.

I still have a few days to think about it. It would be awful in some ways to lose my independence but maybe I am tired of it. Jane bustles in now as she does frequently to see if I'm 'all right'.

I look at her and I think of my trainer Jim's remark at Sandown as we stood saddling Sir Will: 'Struth, where d'you get 'er from? Not yer usual!'